THE BEAST AT THE DOOR

Althea Blue

Supposed Crimes LLC • Matthews, North Carolin

All Rights Reserved
Copyright © 2016 Althea Blue

Published in the United States.

ISBN: 978-1-944591-28-1

www.supposedcrimes.com

This book is typeset in Goudy Old Style.

To my author friends who showed me that real people can actually do this.

CHAPTER ONE

"I WILL not!"

The obstinate expression on the girl's face suggested that she wanted to stamp her foot for emphasis, and only decorum kept her from doing so. Though her posture was perfect, and her clothes impeccable, her demeanor did nothing to conceal the utter horror she felt when she contemplated what her parents had just commanded.

Her mother and father sat before her on chairs as disparate as their appearances. The man, older, balding and running heavily to paunch, sprawled in a large over-stuffed wing-back chair with a thick cushion barely visible beneath his bulk, his legs propped on a matching ottoman casually placed. The woman, more perfectly dressed and complexioned even than her daughter, perched decorously on a hard wooden chair with no padding at all. She wore shades of beige, each layer tailored perfectly to her waspishly-corseted figure, a long string of precisely matched pearls hung around her neck and many diamond rings adorned her elegant fingers, held still and centered on her lap.

The girl resembled her mother closely, pale skin and dark blonde hair tied neatly in a chignon. Her own attire, a light green dress fastened with tiny bone buttons up the back, neatly-shined boots and no visible jewelry, were as simple as fashion allowed, but were elegantly cut and fitted exactly for her frame. Together they presented an imposing picture of a family, and any onlooker would be easily able to place them in the rankings of class that were so important to those from the upper echelons. The girl's expression was the only thing marring the potential family portrait.

"I have made my decision," the man spoke firmly, holding no doubt that he would be obeyed. "The plans will be announced at dinner tonight. You are to smile and be gracious and I will not have any more declarations of disobedience. Do you understand me?"

"And do have Jones assist you into a different dress. That one is far too informal for our guests," her mother added. "We can't have you looking like you just came in from working in the garden."

Involuntarily, Patience glanced down at her immaculate dress, but forced her gaze back to her mother's face. Her own expression now registered betrayal. "But why would you agree without even mentioning it to me? Do my feelings not matter at all? We are talking about my entire life, and I feel I should have some say in my future."

Florence's face didn't shift, but her eye twitched and she nearly looked to her husband for support before taking a deep breath. "Gabriel is an excellent match. He is considered a prime prospect. The Longbranch family has wealth far beyond anything we may imagine; they have more servants than we have rooms. And you cannot deny that he is an attractive young man. I have heard other girls whispering to each other at balls and banquets. We would never choose a husband we did not think you would find acceptable. He is well-groomed and will likely grow into his father's role at the bank once he has proven his training." Florence didn't meet her daughter's eyes.

Patience looked to her father to see what he would say. He always spoke last, and his word was always law. That was a family rule. One she'd recognized even before she could speak herself. If she could change his mind, it wouldn't matter what her mother said.

"Please Father. I am not ready to be married. I've just turned eighteen and there are so many things I hope to do before I become a wife. I want to see the Louvre, and the Champs-Elysees and tour the ruins in Italy. Some young ladies of my acquaintance plan to travel with their chaperones this summer. I wish to go with them and learn something of the world. That will make me a better wife and hostess. Could this not wait a year or two? Then I will marry whoever you choose without question." Patience didn't really mean the last part, but she thought it sounded good. Sometimes a bargain interested her father, as it did many investors.

His face darkened though, and he looked stonily at her. "You will marry whomever I choose at the time I choose it. And that time is now. You will be married in spring. If you wish to travel to the continent on your honeymoon, you can propose the suggestion to Gabriel. He has asked for your hand and I have accepted on your behalf. There will be no more discussion."

Patience made her last-ditch attempt, though she knew it could backfire. "Could we not just wait a little longer? Just to see if Mason returns?" She knew bringing up her lost brother was risky, and that it might be inopportune, but she desperately wished for him at that moment. They hadn't heard anything of him for over a year. Technically they should be wearing mourning and she oughtn't to be able to marry at all, but the war department had not officially declared him dead so it was her father's choice. If he elected not to mourn his oldest son because he was still hoping the boy was alive, Patience had seen no sign of it. They had never gotten along.

If Mason was there, he would never let his baby sister be married off against her will. Not to the likes of Gabriel Longbranch, the biggest bully they'd known in childhood and completely unimproved by achieving adulthood. He was attractive. And clever as well. He likely would succeed his father as Canterbury's most successful head banker, in time.

But he was cruel and used his cleverness as a weapon against those with fewer resources or whom he disliked on a whim. He would do anything to get himself ahead. Patience had heard rumors about the way Gabriel achieved his first place position at Eton, by hiring someone to beat his biggest competition the day before they sat their exams. Gabriel won first place and the other boy had won a broken leg, three broken ribs and a variety of other complaints. No one could prove that Gabriel had orchestrated the altercation, but he wore a smug smile whenever someone mentioned poor Paul Regent, and he never denied it when a schoolmate accused him. And now Patience was to spend her life with this man? It was impossible. Her eyes pleaded with her father, but his face turned red, then purple and he abruptly rose to his feet.

"You will go to your room this instant. You will wait there until you are sent for, at which point you will descend to the dining room to smile and agree with anything suggested to you. You will not speak until spoken to, and then you will keep your answers short. You will smile at Gabriel when I make the announcement to the guests. After dinner you will say goodnight, and then you will return to your room where you will spend the next several days contemplating your duty to your family. If you are well-behaved at dinner tonight, food will be brought to you in your room. If you make any fuss you will be sent to bed immediately like the spoilt child you are and everyone in the dining hall will know that you are too willful to be allowed into polite company. If that happens, I can promise you that the next time you will be seen outside your room will be at your wedding. Do you understand everything I have said?" Her father glared at her with an unyielding expression that Patience recognized to mean a complete lack of exaggeration.

Patience met his gaze and glared right back at him. Then she spun on her heel and marched out of the parlour and up the stairs, shaking with fury.

"I will send Jones up in an hour to help you dress," her mother called out as she left the room.

Patience didn't bother to reply.

CHAPTER TWO

HER FACE blank as Jones dressed her like a child's china doll, Patience tried desperately to think of a way out of her imminent betrothal. She refused to cry in front of Jones or the company she could hear arriving downstairs. Her mind spun as she considered anything that might change her father's mind, though she knew it was most likely already too late. If he'd promised her to Gabriel, he wouldn't be talked out of it, but if there was anything she could say to bribe or blackmail him it would have to be before he made the announcement to the guests. He would never lose face in front of important people. Patience knew her father cared about his reputation far more than he cared about her happiness.

She was the problem child, the youngest of four. Her two older sisters had both married well and moved to different parts of England. As far as

Patience knew they had been given their choice of husbands, but maybe that was just the way it appeared, she couldn't be sure. They were far more biddable than she had ever been; just exactly the proper sort of girls that her parents wanted. They excelled at needlework and pouring tea, and dressed to perfection. Glory was a talented amateur pianist, though her two children now kept her too busy to play. Rose was always perfectly attired; dressing her had been one of their mother's greatest joys. Unlike the other children Patience knew, Rose never had a smudge of dirt on her face, a tear in her stocking, had never even lost a ribbon from her perfectly curled hair.

And then came Patience. Willful from birth, she was smarter by far than her sisters. She resented being stuffed into the restrictive clothing that her sisters seemed to cherish, and had, on more than one occasion, stolen into her brother's room and dressed herself in his outgrown clothes. When she was five she had hacked all her hair off with a knife, because she thought she might want to go to sea and she knew girls couldn't do so. She loved adventure stories and those about pirates and even the history books her brother's tutors forced upon him. Mason and Patience were co-conspirators, he would leave books where she could find them and then cause a distraction so she could have an uninterrupted hour to read or study. In exchange, she helped him prepare for the periodic quizzes his tutors gave and even rewrote some of his essays in her much neater handwriting so he wouldn't have to copy them out himself. The seven years between them didn't mean much, as Patience learned much earlier than he to write clearly and with a better hand.

When Mason left to go to Eton, Patience lost her one ally in the house. Her sisters were two of a kind, and though they were never cruel to her, she didn't have any interest in taking part in their games or talking about eligible gentlemen. Her father was distant and harsh and her mother couldn't figure out where she went wrong with Patience, who never exemplified femininity the way her mother and sisters did. The servants were probably the closest thing she had to friends at home, but though the cook could be counted on for an extra tart or cup of soup when she'd been sent to her room, they hadn't the power to do more without upsetting their employer.

Patience had felt desperately alone since Mason left, and that feeling had only intensified since he joined the British army at the beginning of the Boer conflict. She knew he had enlisted to spite their father, who was waiting for Mason to join him in the investment house. Mason's own talents ran more to creating objects and studying up on new inventions. He wanted to understand everything, and his father wanted to understand nothing more than how to make money. They were like oil and water. Patience had faithfully written to Mason every week, and continued to do so, even though it had been many months since she had received a response. She refused to give up, though. Her immediate fantasy was of him turning up at the door below and saving her from her father's schemes by paying for her to attend London University. Having him home would make all the difference to her; if anyone would stand up to their father on her behalf, it was him.

A sharp rap on her door brought Patience back to the present. She nodded at Jones, who opened the door to the butler, Grayson. "Your father requests your presence downstairs," Grayson informed her with a stiff little bow. He turned to go without waiting for a response.

Patience looked at herself in the mirror. Jones had pinned her hair up into an artful style, and had added a broach to her neckline without her noticing. She nodded in thanks as she noticed that the broach was her only jewelry. The servants had heard more than one argument between Patience and her mother over what Patience considered gaudiness and her mother considered a necessity to be seen in public. Though Patience owned a small casket of jewels she preferred to leave it all in the box and go out with bare neck and fingers. She didn't like the weight or the coldness that jewelry added to her dress, and the simple styles she preferred looked wrong with anything garish to augment them.

She turned to leave her room and was stopped by Jones' whispered reminder to smile. Patience plastered a smile that felt as fake as the two-headed calf she'd once seen when Mason had taken her to a circus. He had paid for her to go on the carousel and took her into the side-show out of his own pocket-money because she'd wanted to see it so badly. She'd loved the carousel but the side show had offended her ten-year-old sensibilities as, she had asserted, anyone with eyes could see that most of the attractions were sewn together, and badly at that. Mason had laughed and bought her popcorn instead.

Jones regarded her attempt with a shake of her head. "Better not smile," she suggested. "Maybe just try not to look so miserable."

Patience shrugged, a very unladylike gesture according to her mother. "I cannot," she stated, turning at the doorway to descend the staircase. *I will attend this dinner as I have no choice, but I cannot look happy about it,* she told herself as she hesitated at the first step. Then she remembered what her father had said. He really would starve her for days if she didn't at least pretend to accede to his wishes. She gathered up every ounce of willpower she had and tried to force a realistic-looking smile onto her face.

As she reached the landing her mother looked her over carefully and nodded once. Patience let out a small sigh. If it was enough to make her mother happy, it would have to do. She accepted a glass of wine from the footman and pretended to take a sip. She didn't really care for wine, but having a glass in hand was a useful foil. If she needed to think about an answer, she could take a sip and it would give her a few seconds. She'd learned that trick from Mason, who hated high-society gatherings even more passionately than Patience. She wished she was still young enough to only suffer through introductions before being sent up to the nursery to have her dinner. Both Glory and Rose had begged to be able to attend the adult dinners from a very young age. Patience was glad not to have to, but when she turned sixteen, she suddenly found that she no longer had the option to hide upstairs. She was expected to help hostess and entertain. Especially once her sisters were married and away from home. Mason could come and go as he liked but Patience was expected to always be available, beautiful, and silent except as necessity demanded. She hated every moment.

She headed for her favorite corner, where she might stand and be sometimes overlooked, but her father pointedly caught her eye and indicated that she should approach him. Suppressing a sigh, Patience turned in his direction and noticed who he was standing with.

"Good evening Mr. Longbranch, Gabriel," she murmured. "Father," she added as an afterthought.

"How wonderful to see you looking so well." Mr. Longbranch announced loudly. "And how excited you must be."

Patience tried to make her smile wider. "Yes sir," she answered. Usually that was enough to satisfy his type. As long as she agreed with him, he would be happy.

Gabriel moved to stand very close to her, so their arms were touching. "How lovely you are, Patience." He smiled, oily charm leaking from every exposed pore. "I'm so terribly glad you accepted my offer."

Patience looked around the room. Had they announced the engagement already? But no one else was looking at her, and there was no one close enough to hear. She tried to inch away from Gabriel but he followed her and there was nothing she could do to escape his touch short of fleeing outright.

"I have put a down payment on a house in town, you will love it. There are seventeen rooms, all the modern conveniences. It will be perfect. We will have to hire servants, of course, but that can wait until the wedding plans are finalized. Of course, Samson will be coming with me as my manservant. And perhaps your father will let you borrow one of your girls, until you get settled and can choose a personal maid," he paused long enough for Patience's father to nod agreement. "And we will have furnishings sent up from London. I will make a trip to choose them personally. Only the best will do." He pushed his chest out and almost strutted like a peacock. He continued extolling his taste in furnishings and servants and Patience let her eyes glaze over.

She nodded whenever he paused for a breath and that seemed to be all he cared about. Her father and Mr. Longbranch wandered elsewhere and her untouched wine glass remained clenched in her hand. For however long it took for Grayson to announce dinner, Gabriel never asked her a single question or paused for her to share an opinion. Patience wondered how long he could talk without taking a break, and decided that he should have been a politician instead of a banker, as he seemed so impressed by the sound of his own voice.

Gabriel took her arm as they approached the dinner table. Of course, he was seated beside her, with her mother on the other side – probably to make sure that Patience didn't say an inappropriate word. She needn't have worried, Patience had no intention of saying anything at all. She wondered if she could make it through the entire dinner without anyone noticing that she didn't speak.

As servants brought around dish after dish, Patience shook her head, refusing most of them. She accepted soup, but barely tasted it, and the roast duck lay untouched on her plate, although it was usually one of her favorite foods.

"And we can summer in Brighton, I have an uncle with a house on the beach." Gabriel continued describing their future together, not noticing that Patience wasn't listening to a word he said.

Finally there were no more courses served and Patience's father rose to his feet. He waited for the quiet conversation to die down and cleared his throat. "I have an announcement to make. It is with greatest pride that I announce the engagement of my youngest daughter to Gabriel Longbranch. Gabriel, Patience, may your marriage be as fulfilling as ours has been." He nodded to his smiling wife at Patience's side. "I wish you long life and prosperity." He raised his wine glass and those seated at the table mimicked the movement. "The wedding will take place in spring, and we hope you all will join us," he finished, sitting back down and drinking the remainder of his wine.

Patience noted that there was no wish for happiness in the toast, and found it surprisingly appropriate. *At least father isn't deluding himself that I might enjoy this union.* She rose with the other women and followed them into the parlour, while the men went to smoke cigars and drink brandy in the games room. Glory grabbed her arm as she entered and pulled her into a corner. She hadn't previously noticed that her sister was there.

"Oh Patience, I am so happy for you. I cannot believe that you will have such an attractive husband. I must admit I am a bit jealous," Glory spoke excitedly. "When I read mother's letter last week I knew I had to be here for the announcement."

"Last week?" Patience asked weakly. "Mother wrote you last week about the engagement?"

"Oh yes." Glory answered. "It must have been Monday or Tuesday. I am so pleased. Do let me help you choose items for your trousseau. I know all the latest styles from Paris, and I am sure Father will allow you to splurge on clothes, just this once."

As if Patience had ever before asked for extravagant clothing. Her usual quarrel with her mother was over wanting simpler and less elaborate clothes, not more. She had a sudden image of dressmakers, pins and dozens of parcels arriving at the door, all for her. The thought made her almost as ill as when she imagined leaving the wedding as Gabriel's bride. Her sister had known about the wedding plans more than a week before Patience had. She wondered who else had known. Had she been the absolute last to be told about her own future. She swallowed hard, trying to suppress both fury and despair, and let her sister natter on. *I will not do it,* she told herself. *There has to be a way out of it. There must be something I can do. Something I can say to make Gabriel not want me. That might be the only way to call it off now. Father will never relent but if Gabriel changes his mind, then perhaps...* She knew Gabriel though, and the man never let something he considered his possession get away from him. He was the same as a child. No one could play with his toys unless he played too, and if he was losing a game he would end the game and stalk off. If it was his, he should always use it best. And she suspected the same principle applied to women.

"I must get out of here." She didn't realize that she'd said the last aloud until Glory looked at her oddly. "I am... not feeling very well," Patience covered. "I would like to sit on the porch for a few minutes."

"Of course," Glory agreed. "The excitement must be too much for you. Let us go sit in the fresh air for a time." She escorted Patience to the front door which Grayson opened for them. The early autumn air was crisp and just a touch cool but it felt good to Patience, who hadn't realized how overheated she was. She sank down into a chair, unmindful of her posture. Glory took the chair next to hers, perched perfectly as usual. If Patience had let Jones tie her corset as tightly as fashion demanded, she wouldn't be able to slouch either, but she had long since come to an agreement with the servants about her intention to breathe, and since she caused them far less work than her sisters did, they were willing to let the protocol slide and not inform her mother.

She stared into the darkness, past the lamps that lit the porch and the driveway. Carriages lined it, with footmen and drivers gathered off to one side, ready to leave whenever their masters wished.

Normally Patience would approach them to make sure they had been fed properly, but for this one night she didn't actually care. Though she turned the problem over and over again, her mind was blank. She could think of nothing she could do or say that would make Gabriel break the engagement. She heard the kitchen door open around the side of the house and some of the maids come out, chattering.

"And she just left? With no notice or anything?" an unfamiliar voice queried.

"When the cook went to wake her in the morning she was just gone," Jones replied. "No one knows where."

"How dreadful. She'll never get another position." The voices faded before Patience could hear anything more, but that was enough. Why hadn't it occurred to her before that she could just leave before the wedding? She knew what time the doors were locked and the servants went to bed. If she gave them time to fall asleep she could be hours away before daylight. *But where will I go?* It couldn't be anywhere they would look for her, her sisters' homes or her aunt and uncle's place in London. She had no close friends who would agree to conceal her and her parents would find her anyway if she stayed in Canterbury. For a moment she debated crossing the Channel and seeing Paris alone, but she discarded that idea as impractical. She didn't have the money it would take to travel properly, nor did she know what papers she would need. It would have to be somewhere in England, but somewhere far away where she wasn't known. She knew there were dozens of small towns and cities isolated from her circle, probably hundreds. Finally she decided it didn't matter exactly where she went, the going was enough. She would leave that night.

The front door opened and people started emerging. "We must join Mother to say goodbye," Glory stood and offered a hand to Patience. "Do you feel better now?"

Patience nodded, "Yes, thank you." She didn't say anything else as she entered the house. Her mother noticed immediately and started to frown but her expression eased when she saw that Patience had been with Glory. She considered Glory a perfect influence who would never do anything inappropriate, no matter how her sister cajoled her. If they had been together than Patience would have been safely guided in a positive direction. She smiled at her youngest, who made a weak attempt to smile back. They said goodbye to all the guests who alighted their carriages and drove away into the night.

Gabriel stayed behind for a moment. "I wanted to say goodbye to you," he told Patience as he tried to lead her into the now-empty parlour.

"My mother prefers that I stay to see all of the guests on their way," Patience replied, the first words she had said to Gabriel since greeting him at the beginning of the evening.

"She won't mind." His grip on her arm grew tighter. "Now that our engagement has been announced we are allowed to be alone together." He said this in a superior tone, as if a professor lecturing his pupil.

Patience knew that Gabriel now felt he had a right to touch her, and her skin crawled with revulsion. "I am very tired, Gabriel. Please let me go. We will talk another time," she said smoothly, hoping that he wouldn't hear the lie in her voice. She had no intention of speaking to him ever again, but she mustn't give herself away now.

He let go as Jones entered the parlour. "I'm sorry sir. I didn't know anyone was in here." She bobbed a curtsy in Gabriel's direction and nodded at Patience.

Seeing the moment as broken, Gabriel exited the room and Patience mouthed a "thank you" in Jones' direction before following him to the front entrance. "Goodnight, Gabriel," she said, as she stepped beside her mother, who was saying goodnight to Mr. Longbranch. Gabriel nodded back to her as he followed his father to their carriage, the last one waiting to leave. Grayson closed the door behind them and Patience's father nodded in satisfaction as he lost sight of the pair.

"Excellent dinner, dear," he commented to Patience's mother, as if she had had anything to do with the preparation for the party. Patience had never heard him thank the servants for their work, but he always thanked his wife. It was all about protocol to him. He would never do or say anything that could be viewed as gratitude outside his class and it made Patience wonder if her mother had ever thought of fleeing her own wedding. Unlikely, she decided. Her mother was born for this role.

She turned to her mother to excuse herself. "I am feeling quite tired. May I go upstairs now?" she asked.

"Go ahead. You did well this evening. Everyone said what a beautiful woman you have grown into. All our friends are looking forward to the wedding."

Patience wondered if her mother had even noticed how little she ate, or that she hadn't said a word at the dinner table. If she had, she probably would have considered it perfectly ladylike. Everyone else may be looking forward to the wedding, but they would be disappointed one and all. For the first time since she'd been called into the parlour that afternoon, Patience felt like she could breathe. She thanked her mother and quickly ascended the stairs, waiting impatiently for Jones to come and undress her so she could start making preparations.

CHAPTER THREE

LYING IN bed, Patience tried to think of all the things she would need when she left the house. She had never been anywhere by herself and she hadn't the faintest idea how to start packing.

Rolling off her bed she lit a candle and went to her wardrobe, opening the doors and staring in dismay at the array of dresses. Most of them would be impossible for her to put on by herself, and were completely unsuitable for anything more strenuous than sitting at the opera or a dinner party. She found one light grey dress with buttons up the front and pulled it from its hanger, tossing it carelessly onto the bed.

For a moment she wondered if she could sneak into Mason's room and find something of his to wear, but she didn't know how to act like a boy and would give herself away in moments. None of the dresses were very warm, the winter clothes had not yet been brought out as autumn was just starting to announce its chill. She added a dark blue shawl and several petticoats and bloomers to the pile. She found her stoutest pair of boots, though they were still more delicate than she would prefer, and then looked around the room for what else might be needed.

Her eyes caught on her jewelry casket. She rummaged through it until she found her favorite pearls, which had once belonged to a grandmother Patience could barely remember. What little money she had was in her reticule and she added that to the pile. She wondered which hat would be appropriate for running away, and finally chose a simple straw boater. Pulling stockings from her drawer she quickly drew off the long nightdress and replaced it with the underclothes. Automatically her hand reached out for her corset, but she dropped it again immediately. Without Jones there was no way she could tighten it, and since this was her one chance at freedom, she decided that wearing a corset would be an unnecessary constraint. Without the binding garment the dress was slightly too tight, but not by much, since her refusal to wear properly tightened corsets even when meeting the dressmakers meant it was sized fairly accurately. She felt grateful for that, enough to make up for years of listening to their displeasure.

She searched her room for a bag to carry her extra things in and came up empty. There were trunks and suitcases in the closet under the stairs but she wouldn't be able to carry one, even if she could retrieve it without being heard. Then she remembered playing at traveling with her sisters when they were children. There was an old carpetbag in the nursery cupboard that they used to fill with their precious things and pretend to go on a journey. The nursery was right next door. The servants had been in bed for nearly an hour so it should be safe. She opened her door a crack, listening for any out-of-place sound. She heard nothing, though she made herself wait a full minute before she crept into the nursery with her candle and found the bag, just where she remembered it residing, on the shelf in the cupboard. Quickly returning to her room she stuffed her things in the bag, picked up her shoes and blew out the candle.

Hugging the wall, she tiptoed to the stairs, avoiding the one step she knew creaked whenever the smallest weight was placed on it, and reached the bottom without a sound. There was no light shining in the front hall, but she had grown up in the house and knew it well from numerous games of hide and seek and blind man's bluff when she was small. She had to put her bag down to reach the latch near the top of the front door, pulling it gently open without a squeak. She thanked god for servants who kept every hinge oiled, as she exited the house and closed it softly behind her.

Patience knew that the first servant awake was usually the cook, who might never enter the front hall to notice that the door was unlatched. She might have as many as six or seven hours before her departure was observed. She quickly laced her boots on her feet, grabbed her bag and walked down the drive. Once there she had the first decision to make. If she turned left, the street would lead into Canterbury proper, where there might be people still around. No one who was likely to know her, but men leaving the taverns and other lowlifes might bother her. If she turned right, it would be many miles before she reached another village. She couldn't remember exactly what lay that way, but that's the road she took. Better to face the real unknown as soon as possible.

The night was dark and cooler than she had expected. She hugged the shawl to her and swapped the hand that held the carpet bag. Very quickly, Patience's feet started to hurt but she ignored them and strode as quickly as possible, lighted by only a crescent moon. A few times she tripped over something unexpected in the road, but she caught herself each time. Her stomach reminded her that she had barely eaten since noon and she regretted not stopping in the kitchen to fill up her bag with food. That would have been risky though. The cook would surely have heard her, as she slept in a small room off the pantry and Patience had heard one of the servants say was a restless sleeper.

At some point she saw what she thought might be apple trees just off the road. She wandered over to them and felt for low branches. Sure enough, there were small apples hanging from the branch. She twisted one off and bit into it. It was sour and not quite ripe, but she didn't care. She finished the apple and took another. Then she took as many as she could reach and put them in her bag. They weren't numerous, most would be on higher branches and she didn't dare risk climbing the tree in the dark. She hoped she could find more food if she continued walking and returned to the road.

Patience could no longer feel her feet. She wondered if that was going to be a problem, but at least they weren't hurting anymore. She forced herself to keep going, though her eyes burned and her head ached from lack of sleep. She knew if she stopped this close to home she would be found easily and would never be given a second chance to flee. Her father was more than capable of locking her in her room until the wedding. With that thought she quickened her pace and started to think about where she might hide. Whenever she passed a crossroad, she always turned down it, making sure she was still heading in the same general direction, away from Canterbury.

She knew how to find the North Star and keep following it, another lesson from her brother, who was fascinated by the movement of the stars. He told her that this star would always point the way if she was lost, and told her stories about American slaves who escaped to Canada using the same star, before the War Between the States set them free. Her favorite story had been about Harriet Tubman, a woman who managed not only to escape the south, but also returned to help other slaves escape. Patience thought her life was a bit like a slave's. Not that she ever had to work, but in that she had no choices to make for herself. Slaves were married against their will, just like Patience would be if she didn't escape. She began to pretend to be Harriet and think about what she would do to stay free. Harriet had stolen food, hidden during the day and run at night, just like Patience was doing.

After what felt like several days' worth of walking, the eastern sky started to lighten. Patience realized she could see details she'd been missing before. Any time now one of the servants would notice the front door was unbolted and would wake her father to tell him. Probably no more than a few minutes after that they would discover she was gone. It would take them a while to come after her, but she should be well hidden within the hour. With that in mind, she left the main road, following a small path into a farmer's field. She needed somewhere that no one would discover her, but where she'd be protected from the sun and from any animals that might be nosing around. She dismissed the first barn she came to, as it looked well-used and people would be in and out. A second barn housed horses, and cows who were already lowing with their udders full of milk.

She quickened her speed, ignoring the sharper pains that seemed to increase with each step. She came to a small structure that she didn't recognize at first. It was too small for a barn or a granary or even a smokehouse. Then she realized there were no windows and only one sturdy door. The structure was all stone, no wood, and she decided it must be an ice house. Her sister had an ice house and this late in the season there was hardly ever ice left. Patience crept to the door and looked around quickly, to see if anyone was around. Seeing no one, she quickly lifted the latch and checked the back of the door to make sure there was also a latch there. It would do her no good to lock herself in; no one would ever hear a call for help.

Before she closed the door behind her she looked around the room. As she had suspected, there was only a tiny pile of ice under a piece of burlap in the corner nearest the door. The rest of the room had straw covering the floor and several large pieces of burlap in a pile in the furthest corner. With the door closed there was only the tiniest bit of light visible from underneath, where it didn't quite meet the frame. At least Patience would be able to tell when night fell. She went to the pile of burlap, rolled up one piece to make a pillow and used another piece as a blanket. The rest of it made quite a nice nest for her to curl up in. As long as no one needed any ice that day she would be fine.

Though exhausted, Patience couldn't seem to fall asleep. She had never slept on anything less comfortable than a featherbed, and though the pile of sacking was an improvement over hard ground, it was nowhere near soft. Every sharp pebble or hump on the dirt floor jabbed into her back, no matter how she tried to smooth it out. It was chilly in the ice house, and her shawl wasn't nearly the protection that an eiderdown quilt would have offered. Though she could hear no birds from inside the thick-walled structure, there were unexplained sounds coming from outside, made eerie and echoing by the room she inhabited. She dozed on and off, but awoke frequently thinking she heard someone entering the hut. Her stomach was also hurting, and she wasn't sure if it was from lack of food, or whether eating apples before they were ripe was a bad idea. All in all, by the time dusk fell she was more tired than she'd been before she stopped for the day.

She carefully opened the door and listened to see if she could hear anyone moving around. There was a cow mooing from the direction of the barn she'd passed the night before, but she heard nothing else. She eased the door open, slipped out and carefully closed it behind her. She couldn't find a road but walked through the field that lay to her left. She thought that was north, though the stars weren't visible behind thick clouds. Without a road to follow she moved slower than she had the night before, but she figured it didn't matter since she'd be harder to find.

She passed through a series of fields, some with crops almost ripe for harvesting, others already gleaned of their foodstuffs. She found a small patch of woods where she recognized some blackberry bushes with fruit still clinging to their branches. She picked and ate as quickly as she could and once she was full stripped the bushes bare. She was feeling a bit dizzy and realized how long it had been since she'd had anything to drink. There was a tiny stream in the woods, barely a trickle. She sat beside it, drinking handful after handful of water until her stomach was full to bursting. She wished hard that she had planned her escape more thoroughly. She berated herself for not taking a few days to consider what she'd need and collect it before she fled.

She didn't for a moment consider going back, and probably would never be able to find her way even if she wanted to, but she had always prided herself on being clever and the first time that cleverness was tested she had failed miserably. Sitting beside the stream she started to cry, her tears falling into the water and rushing towards the unknown. For some reason, thinking about the freedom of her tears made her feel better. She purposefully straightened her back, thrust her shoulders into place and stood up, marching with a new energy. This feeling lasted long enough to see her through the woods and into another field. At the end of the field was another barn, one with animals on the ground floor and a hayloft above. Gratefully Patience climbed the ladder into the hayloft, dug herself a bed into a pile of hay and fell into a dreamless sleep.

The crowing of a rooster shattered her slumber and she quickly climbed out of the barn and went on her way before the farmer could find her. This pattern lasted for two more nights, Patience would walk through the day, find a barn to sleep in and repeat the process. She was exhausted, her feet burned and blisters formed, broke, and reformed, but she continued.

One day she found an orchard with apples that were riper than the first ones. Feeling only slightly guilty she took as many as she could carry. Occasionally, she would come to a small village where she would drink her fill at a well and do her best to wash her exposed skin and tidy her hair. She knew she looked a fright, one of the many things she'd forgotten to bring was a comb, but she used twigs to tease most of the tangles out and braided her hair tightly with a ribbon she'd found in the dirt. She no longer worried about being caught by her family, she doubted they'd recognize her if they saw her. Her problems were reduced to finding food and water and a place to sleep.

When she climbed into a barn loft on her fourth night she was surprised to find someone already sleeping in it. Nervously she started to head back down the ladder but the form jerked awake holding a knife.

Patience scrambled down the ladder and tried to run but he jumped down in front of her. "And who might you be?" the man asked.

Patience looked to the door he was blocking with his body and looked back at the knife he held in front of him. "I did not mean to disturb your rest. I am only a traveler and mean no harm. I was looking for a place to sleep but I am quite happy to find another one." She tried to edge around him.

The man moved to block her. He was older than Patience, maybe around her father's age, with a dirty, tangled beard and torn and filthy clothing. There was something wrong with his face, it seemed twisted on one side, maybe a scar or some pox from long ago. There was no sense of kindness from him.

Her fears were confirmed when the man spoke again. "Here is a right good place for you to sleep. We can have a little fun." She didn't need to see the licentious leer on his face to know what he meant by fun. Her heart raced faster and her eyes darted around, seeking an escape route.

"I believe I will keep walking a while longer. I have fallen behind today and my friends will be waiting for me." She tried to keep her voice steady but was betrayed by a noticeable quiver. Still, she stood with a straight back, clutching her bag tightly.

The man spat in the dirt. "What friends? I don't think anyone will miss you for a few hours." He advanced toward her and Patience retreated until her back was against the wall. He kept moving toward her, keeping the knife between them. Patience started to hyperventilate, even as her mind raced to find a way out. She could scream for help, but she didn't know if anyone would hear her, or come to her assistance if they did. The people in the house might be as bad as the man in front of her. If she didn't get away, she knew what would happen and she wasn't willing to let it.

Suddenly she took one big step forward, swung her bag at the man's head and ran as soon as she let go. She darted out the barn door, leaving it open in her wake and fled headlong into the closest field. She didn't stop to think about her direction, or move quietly, she just ran. Her lungs burned, a stitch formed in her side and got worse and worse and she kept running. She didn't stop until she was hopelessly lost and exhausted. She had to lean against a tree, her breath coming in gasps that hurt each time she inhaled. Her hands shook and she burst into tears, crying into the unforgiving bark until she had no moisture left in her.

Crying didn't make her feel better, just more vulnerable. She'd lost everything she had. Her changes of clothes, her memories of home, even her few remaining apples. She had even lost her shawl, which had been tied around the bag's straps as the night was a warm one. She literally had nothing but the clothes on her back and she felt completely used up. Sliding down the tree she curled into as small a ball as she could and shook until sleep overcame her.

CHAPTER FOUR

WHEN PATIENCE awoke she felt scared and very small. She looked around her and noted that she was in a forest, but she had no idea how deep into it or in what direction she'd come from. She debated just staying where she was, but hunger and thirst eventually overcame fear and she stood shakily, clutching the tree for support. She couldn't hear anything that suggested water nearby and the light that filtered through the tall trees was diffused and greenish, giving everything a slightly spooky cast. There were no trees with fruit and no bushes with berries so she wandered aimlessly around the forest searching for a path of any kind. Even an animal's trail would lead to water eventually, on one end or another, she knew that, but she couldn't find evidence of anything larger than a rabbit. The undergrowth was thick and smelled slightly moldy and she wondered if any people had ever been in this wood at all. Maybe she was the first to explore it.

That made her feel slightly braver and she continued watching the ground in hopes of discovering water. She was so intent on the details that she didn't notice when the woods thinned out until she was entirely free of the trees. Suddenly noticing her lack of cover she retreated and hid behind a large oak, peering around. There was a thin strip of some kind of grass that reached about knee high and then a tall stone fence. It went on quite a ways, with no breaks or gates that she could see. Near the place where the wall turned away from the woods she saw that it had crumbled, just a little at the top. Carefully looking up and down, and seeing no one, Patience went as far as she could in the cover of the trees and then raced to the wall, pressing herself against it and letting her heart rate slow to normal. She tried to climb the wall, and although the rough texture suggested that it should be easy to climb, she found it impossible to find a foothold with her boots.

Remembering childhood adventures climbing trees while her parents were away and couldn't scold her, she removed her boots, tied them together and strung them around her neck. Her stocking feet had no trouble finding cracks in the stone and she pulled herself up just high enough that she could peek through the gap left by the crumbling wall.

The first thing Patience noticed was a large house. Not quite as large as the one she'd fled, but certainly more sizable than anything she'd seen in the villages she passed through. Windows were uniformly covered by curtains and the door that led inside was firmly shut. Letting her gaze wander, Patience saw a large garden, filled with food she recognized from the garden at home. Her stomach rumbled with the reminder that she had barely eaten for many days, but she was still cautious. What finally drove her over the wall was the enticement of a well between the back door and the first row of vegetables. She pulled herself to the top of the wall and quickly crept her way down to the ground, hoping that no one in the house was peering through the windows just then. When she reached the grass she paused, waiting for a window or door to open and reveal a housewife with a broom or dogs to chase her away, but nothing happened. She crept around the inside of the wall until she was at the closest point to the well.

Patience drew up a bucket full of water and crouched behind the well, believing herself hidden from the house. She drank until she could hold no more and then looked longingly at the growing vegetables. *It's stealing,* she told herself. *So was taking the fruit from the orchards,* her stomach argued back. She didn't really have a good rejoinder for that. She hadn't exactly thought of it as stealing when she was taking the apples, because there were so many more, but that's what it was.

Thieves were regarded as one of the lowest forms of criminals, in Patience's world. She'd never stopped to consider that maybe people were just stealing because they were hungry, rather than out of criminal intent. Now that she was one of the hungry ones, her upbringing was brought sharply into contrast with the needs of her body. *If I just take a little, maybe no one will notice.* She quickly pulled a few carrots and parsnips, storing them in the bodice of her dress, and retraced her path along the fence until she reached the crumbled corner.

She was up and over the wall again before she had time for second thoughts and returned to the safety of the woods where she sat against a tree and pulled the food from her dress. Without more than cursorily brushing off the dirt she ate everything she had stolen and felt less guilty with every swallow. She told herself that it was all right if she didn't do it again and spent the rest of the day near the edge of the woods, neither leaving their shelter, nor straying too far from that stone wall.

CHAPTER FIVE

THE NEXT morning, she found herself staring at the wall again. She remained cautious and held out as long as she could, but a source of food so close was too tempting to resist. She followed the same pattern as the day before, drinking her fill before ravaging a different area of the garden and running with her ill-gotten gains. The third day she didn't even have to talk herself into it. She just climbed over and down and was less careful to stay against the wall. She was just letting the bucket fall back into the well when a terrible roaring came from around the side of the house.

Patience dropped the bucket and froze, crouching behind the wall of the well, positive some animal was coming to devour her. She shook in fear, unable to decide whether to run for it or to stay hidden, as meager a protection as the well might provide. The roar came again and again, but it didn't seem to be getting any closer. Maybe it wasn't inside the grounds. If it was outside the wall, Patience didn't want to risk leaving the safety of the garden. But if it was here, she didn't want to stay. Moving slowly, and ready to run if anything came near her, Patience peeked around the side of the house.

She could just make out a ground-floor window open and something inside the house which occasionally leaned over the sill so she could just see the edge of it. She didn't know what it was, it was far too big to be a dog or even a bear. The roaring continued regularly, and was definitely coming from the creature. A very small part of Patience wanted to see it better and she found herself edging out from the protection of the wall, only by a few inches. She stared at the thing and still couldn't recognize it as anything from her brother's books on animals. Certainly it was nothing from England. Maybe from Africa or India. Perhaps whoever lived in the house had chained it up as a prize. She knew men who had gone large-game hunting, and though they came back with trophies instead of live animals she supposed it might happen.

Forgetting that she needed to stay hidden in her curiosity, she was nearly around the corner of the house. From this angle the beast looked like nothing more than a wolf, but standing upright and taller than the largest man she had ever seen. When its head swung in her direction and it roared again Patience jumped back involuntarily and tripped over something lying behind her. She landed hard on her rear and let out a tiny cry before she could stop herself. Desperately she looked toward the beast but it wasn't turned toward her anymore.

She thought she was safe and was crawling back towards the garden when she saw a flicker of movement in a window directly above the beast. It might have been nothing, a trick of the light but it might also have been the twitch of a curtain caused by someone looking through a gap. Realizing that she was in full view of anyone who happened to glance her way, she stood and fled back through the garden, hoisting herself up over the wall in haste, and didn't slow until she was safely back in her woods. It wasn't until that point that she realized she'd dropped her boots when she fell, and her stomach reminded her that she hadn't picked any vegetables to eat, but her fear determined that she wasn't going anywhere near that house again to fetch either food or shoes.

That night the cramping in her stomach was only a slight distraction from the raging storm that blew stinging rain into her eyes and across her exposed skin. She huddled in a pile under some fallen branches and waited for the storm to pass but it showed no signs of slowing.

Patience couldn't feel her hands or her feet. Her dress was a sodden mass of fabric and the ground under her a swampland of mud. Every time a lightning bolt lit the sky she was positive it was going to hit the tree she was trying to shelter under, and her teeth were chattering so loudly she could hear them over the storm. Eventually, half-frozen and fully-exhausted she decided that being eaten would be a better fate than dying of hypothermia in a nameless forest somewhere in the middle of England. She found her way to the fence easily enough, but climbing the wall took her several tries, as she couldn't feel her fingers or toes and kept slipping when she thought she had a safe perch. Finally she made it over the top and almost tumbled down the inside. She wasn't hurt but it took her a few minutes to gather her strength enough to stand and drag herself to the back door.

Of course it was locked tight and there was no give to it at all. She wished she had been born a thief so she knew how to get inside a locked house, but she didn't have a clue. She tried each window in turn, but they were latched as tightly as the door. The corner of the house drew her attention, where she'd gone to look at the beast. She cautiously edged around the bricks, listening for any sign of the creature or any other inhabitants of the home. The first window was shut as tightly as the ones around back, but the one from which the animal had roared was unlatched. She peeked inside but it was pitch black and she couldn't see if there was anything in the room. Screwing up all the courage she could muster, Patience slid the window open a little at a time and pulled herself over the sill.

Her stocking-clad feet hardly made a sound as they landed on the floor and she dropped into a crouch, peering around the room. A flash of lightening illuminated the space and she felt sure that nothing more than furniture occupied it. Huddling against the wall, Patience willed her body to stop shaking and warm up. The room wasn't that much warmer than the outside, but at least no rain was pounding on her head. While she waited, hoping to dry off a little or for the rain to stop, she heard the same roaring as before. She jumped at the sound and looked around but the creature was clearly not in the room with her.

The door to the corridor was slightly open and she moved closer to it, listening and trying to determine how far away the creature was. The roar came again, and she was sure it wasn't getting any closer. She heard nothing else and some nonsensical part of her wanted to see the beast again. She left the room and padded lightly down the hall in the direction from which the sound came. There were no creaks from the floor but she worried that she was leaving a trail of droplets behind her. Patience wished there was somewhere that she could wring out her clothes and her hair, which was still dripping into her eyes. She tried to push the water away using a sodden sleeve but it made no noticeable difference.

She jumped again when the roar sounded but was able to pinpoint the origin as a room just ahead. The door was slightly open and there was a faint glow coming from inside. Patience stared at it. She might have expected to see a flickering, as from a candle or a gas lamp but this light was steady and she recognized it as electric. A few of the wealthiest families she knew had installed electric lights, but she wondered who was providing power in a remote area like this.

Beyond the source of the light, a huge creature

stood, looking out the window. It paced a few meters, turned back to the window and roared again. This close she could feel the power of the sound through her chest and it made her freeze. A small rational part of her screamed to flee, but she was fascinated by the creature. From the back it could have been a bear, shaggy fur covered it entirely, but when it turned its head a little she could see that the snout wasn't like anything she'd seen before. It didn't really resemble a wolf at all, though that was what she'd thought earlier in the day, maybe it was closer to a gorilla. It certainly belonged to no species she knew of.

It reminded her of a story she'd once heard from the Americas about something called Bigfoot, but that was just a tale told by silly people. Its eyes were bright and its head moved smoothly in her direction. Patience realized that it was looking at her and she froze, too scared to run. She berated herself for ever coming back to this house and she waited for the thing to come at her, but it didn't. It turned away and continued pacing and roaring.

Patience backed out of the room slowly, trying to keep silent. Why hadn't it come after her? Was it blind? Shouldn't it have been able to smell her at least? Her brother's biology tutor had been very definite that animals had a much greater sense of smell than humans, and often used that sense to hunt out prey. Maybe it didn't consider a girl prey. Maybe it didn't like the taste. Patience shuddered with the thought that it might have enough intelligence to realize what species she was and that she wasn't food. Then she berated herself again for jumping to conclusions. She had no idea why it hadn't come after her, she should simply be grateful that it hadn't.

Passing the room she'd emerged from she took another glance out the window. It was still open and she walked toward it, meaning to exit the house and return to the woods. She heard the rain lashing down and realized she was still shivering badly. If she left the vague safety of the house she'd be likely to end up sick, and there was no one to take care of her. She closed the window nearly all the way and went out to the corridor again. She listened but could hear nothing more than the beast's occasional roar. Did no one else inhabit the home? From what she could make out in the darkness it looked clean. There was no smell of mold, rot or even dust, so either people had been here recently, or the creature had taken up housework.

Patience almost laughed aloud at the thought of the huge beast with a broom in one hand and a mop in the other.

She came to a flight of stairs and climbed carefully up, keeping to the sides of the steps where they were less likely to creak under her weight. On the first floor there was a steady, pale light glowing in the hallway; enough to illuminate a row of doors on both sides. Most of the doors were closed tightly, but a few stood ajar. As she passed, Patience peered into each room. She saw a music room, with a piano in the center and a harp to one side. There was a sort of parlour, with several sofas and chairs around the large space. A few rooms had sheets draped over whatever lay inside, probably unused bedrooms. Finally, at the very end she came to a beautifully-stocked library.

There were more lights in that room, though the fireplace was cold. Forgetting herself, Patience entered and stood in the center, slowly spinning around and letting her eyes take in the rows and rows of leather-bound books that sat neatly on shelves, piled on tables, stacked wherever there was room.

Patience had never seen so many books. Her parents did not believe that girls should spend their time reading. "It spoils the eyes and the disposition," Patience heard in her mother's voice, a phrase that had been oft repeated in her childhood whenever she was caught with her brother's books. Mason had a fairly decent collection, and although he wasn't terribly interested in fiction, he'd pretended a love for the adventure stories that Patience craved to encourage their father to purchase them.

Patience would read hidden in closets, under her bed, wherever her sisters wouldn't find her and carry the transgression back to their mother. Mason let her hide in his room quite often, he'd even created a hinged side panel in his wardrobe that could be propped open to let in light. He was very clever with his hands, although their father discouraged that skill for his only son and heir. "Gentlemen do not get their hands dirty," was the only phrase in the household that may have been used more frequently than the one about girls not reading. Neither of the children was willing to be kept from activities they loved, no matter how many times they were punished for them.

Patience couldn't help herself. She floated to the nearest bookshelf and let her fingers run over the spines, reading the titles one by one. There were more books than she could ever read, maybe more books than she could even touch but she would do almost anything to be given the chance to try.

She pulled out a single volume, *David Copperfield*. It was a book she had loved as a child. Forgetting where she was and who else might share the house, Patience held the book, feeling a sense of loss. Her childhood, unpleasant as parts of it had been, was now definitely over and she longed to recapture just a modicum of the safety she had felt when she was too young for the worst of the fights over being a 'young lady' to have started. The craving to lose herself in a story and live with the characters, forgetting everything else for a time was too compelling.

Patience had the presence of mind not to curl up in one of the big leather chairs, as she might have done at home, but made herself a space on the floor behind one of them and opened the book. The pages had been neatly cut, so someone had probably read this before her and she spared a moment to wonder who it had been, before letting her eyes caress the first words. Immediately she was transported out of the library, away from her soaked and ruined clothes and into the life of the young protagonist. So far into the story she fell that when her eyes closed between one page turn and the next, she dreamt of David and knew herself no more.

CHAPTER SIX

SOMETHING FEELS *wrong.* Her fuzzy brain was not quite sure what it was. She felt a hard surface under her, nothing like a bed. Why was she sleeping on the floor? She was also colder than she could remember being, possibly ever. The thought started her shivering again. She slowly opened her eyes and saw that she was indeed lying on a floor, and not one she recognized. Blinking repeatedly she tried to focus her eyes and remember where she was. Her head hurt and she couldn't seem to think how she'd come to be there. She felt a book in her hand, and that was familiar at least. She'd often fallen asleep reading before, but somehow this still didn't seem right. Rolling her neck, which popped alarmingly, she raised her gaze from the wooden floor and found a girl staring at her.

The girl wore a simple gown, loose and narrow with no evidence of corset or proper petticoats. Why was she looking at Patience? She managed to look both surprised and cross. Patience tried to identify her and failed; as far as she knew she'd never seen the girl before. Patience's shivering increased and she realized that her dress was damp. Suddenly it all came back to her. The storm, the roaring creature, the library and *David Copperfield*, still in her hands. She jerked to a sitting position, suddenly wide awake and terrified. The girl didn't look threatening, but Patience had lost a lot of trust in people over the last few days.

"Who are you?" Patience asked, tentatively.

The girl blinked in surprise. "I'm Ada. What are you doing here? You can't be here, you have to go!" The words ran over each other as if Ada was trying to rush through them without thinking.

Patience examined Ada's dress again and decided she must be a servant, though what kind of creature needed a servant she had no idea. Maybe she was the servant of the beast's owner. While she was processing that thought, Ada spoke again, even more quickly but with more force. "You can't be here. It's not safe. Please go away."

Patience thought about it. "I have nowhere to go. That is why I breached your hospitality. The rain was too heavy."

The girl, Ada, shook her head quickly. "It's not safe for you to be here," she repeated.

"Because of the creature?" Patience asked.

Ada blanched. "Yes. Because of the creature. He has a terrible temper. He hates people being here and he always kills them to eat."

Patience noted the pronoun. "He has not eaten you," she pointed out.

"I'm not... He won't hurt me. But other people are different. He doesn't like to be bothered. Please just go."

Patience felt at a disadvantage with Ada standing over her, so she stood too. She swayed a little on reaching her feet but bit the inside of her cheek and stayed upright. Automatically her hands moved to smooth her skirt into tidiness, but she knew it was a lost cause. She tried to ignore her bedraggled state and stood with a straight back, feet planted firmly. "I wish to seek employment, then. Please direct me to your employer. I can be a lady's maid, or even a general housemaid." Patience had no idea how to manage either position, but she figured she'd pick it up as she went.

Ada blinked at her. "My... employer?" she asked. The girl seemed a little slow.

"The person for whom you work? I am seeking employment as a servant." Patience's voice was firm, yet gentle. Really, there was no need to tax the girl's mind. If she was the only servant in a house this size, and Patience had seen no sign of anyone else, then there would certainly be work for her. As long as they didn't look too closely at her dress. "As you can see, I was caught in the storm but if you can lend me a needle and thread, I can certainly put my dress to right before I see the owner of the house." She looked hopefully at Ada, waiting for her to agree. She had learned that tone of voice from her mother, and no one ever questioned her mother when she used it.

The girl looked taken aback, although by what Patience wasn't sure. "Oh yes, my employers. Well, they aren't home right now, but they are definitely not looking for another servant so if you will just follow me to the door, I will show you out. The rain has mostly stopped now and you will be fine on the remainder of your journey."

Patience felt all the fire drain out of her, along with what little hope she'd had for finding somewhere to stay. Every part of her hurt, her head was pounding and her vision was starting to swim again. It took everything she had to remain standing. "Please," she whispered. "I have nowhere else to go and it is so c-cold."

Ada examined her more closely. "But the creature..." she made one more attempt at protest.

"Please. He knows I'm here already. He saw me but did not injure me. So it is fine. I promise I will not blame you if I get eaten. Just for a while. Until I get warm." Tears sprang unbidden to her eyes and she pushed them away with the heels of her hands. Crying never solved anything and she never cried in front of a servant. Even if she was to be one herself.

Ada nodded decisively. "You can stay until morning. Then we will see. Follow me."

The girl did not have the manner of a servant, Patience thought. Where she had grown up servants didn't argue with their betters, nor did they order them around. But then Patience didn't look like the wealthy daughter of an investor anymore. She didn't even look like a servant.

Not having seen a mirror for several days, she

suspected she looked more like a beggar woman. There was nothing she could do about her dress or her hair at the moment, but she could definitely affect her manner. She drew up until her back was ramrod straight and pushed her shoulders back, remembering the hated lessons in deportment she had been subjected to as a child. That was one tutor her parents hadn't argued over hiring for her. At the time she'd wished desperately to learn anything else, but now the training on presenting a good face no matter the situation was very helpful.

She tried as hard as she could to stop shivering and ignored the black spots that floated around the edges of her vision. She focused her gaze on Ada's back and followed her into the corridor, down the stairs, and into a warm kitchen. It wasn't until she was seated at a scarred wooden table that Patience realized she was still clutching the copy of *David Copperfield* from the library. Carefully she placed it on the table and pushed it away, so Ada would know she didn't mean to steal it. Then she turned toward the fireplace and thrust her hands out as if to clutch at the faint warmth.

"You should take your chair closer to the fire," Ada suggested, "so you'll warm up faster."

Patience lost no time moving herself so close to the fire that, were her skirts less damp, they would likely be scorched. The fierce heat felt wonderful on her face and hands, and she could see steam rising from her clothes as they started to dry.

Ada observed the steam. "That's not going to work very well, one moment." She ducked out of the room and came back with a heavy wool cloak. "You'd better take everything off so it can dry properly. You can wear this and we will hang the rest on the racks so they dry faster." She handed the cloak to Patience and turned her back, fussing with moving a rack in front of the fire.

Patience was quite shocked. Undressing in a kitchen seemed indecent, especially as she didn't know who else inhabited the house. Ada's presence didn't bother her, but what if a man came in while she was wearing nothing but a cloak? Impossible.

As if Ada sensed what she was thinking she spoke again. "There's no one else here. Just us. And the creature, of course," she added as an afterthought. "But he won't come in here, I promise."

Thinking longingly of being actually warm and having dry clothes to cover her, Patience pushed her objections to the side and quickly removed her dress and underthings, stepping out of them and fastening the cloak at her throat. She held it together with one hand as she gathered her clothes with the other and lay them anywhere they seemed likely to dry. Then she sank back in the hard chair and let the fire toast her face and bare feet. Her boots were still missing, but she decided not to think about them for the time being and just focus on getting warm.

Even with the fire built up under Ada's sure hands, Patience was still shivering fiercely. When Ada thrust a mug full of what looked like soup into her hands they closed around it but she had to focus carefully so as not to spill as she brought it to her mouth. The hot soup burned her throat as she swallowed without waiting for it to cool, but despite the pain, the first taste reminded her stomach of how little she'd had to eat since she left home. She barely took the time to breathe as she finished the soup in unladylike gulps. Ada watched incredulously as she emptied the cup in mere moments, but didn't comment as she retrieved the mug and filled it a second time.

When that cup was gone too, Patience suddenly remembered her manners. Speaking through teeth that still wanted to chatter, despite the warm food and the fire, she raised her eyes to meet Ada's. "Thank you," she said, truly grateful for the girl's help. "It's very good."

"Do you want more?" Ada asked, still looking at Patience.

She blushed. No lady ever accepted second helpings much less third, but her stomach was still growling and her hands still shook. "If it would not be too much trouble," she responded weakly.

A third cup of soup was offered to her, as well as a large hunk of brown bread. As Patience ate, Ada's gaze never left her face. She looked worried, though Patience wasn't sure if she was worried about her or only about her master catching her serving food to a strange girl.

"You can stay for tonight only. I'll prepare a bath and make up a bed for you, and find you nightclothes, since it doesn't look like your dress will be dry very soon. In the morning I'll make breakfast and you can be on your way."

Patience nodded agreement. At that point she

would have agreed to anything in order to stay in the nice warm house for a little longer. She still had no intention of leaving in the morning, but it would give her longer to work on Ada and convince her that Patience could help.

Ada retrieved a large metal tub from a side room, as Patience finished her bread. She went to a strange contraption in the corner, attached a tube to one of three metal pipes and placed the other end of it in the tub. Then she began to turn a handle. For a minute nothing happened, but then water started flowing from the tube into the tub. Patience stared in amazement at the system. It didn't look like any hand pump she had seen before, the flow of water was steady and Ada didn't seem to have to strain as she turned the crank. Amazement turned to astonishment as Patience noticed the steam rising from the water. The water was coming out hot! How was that possible? In only a few minutes the water was nearing the top of the tub and Ada stopped cranking to stick a finger in and test the temperature. She frowned slightly, moved the tube to a different pipe and added more water. Testing it again, she smiled. It was the first time Patience had seen the girl smile and she suddenly realized that she was beautiful.

Her entirely-plain dress, lack of ornamentation, and messily-braided dark curls had masked it before, but now that Patience really looked at her, she was astounded. She far outshone the china dolls of Patience's acquaintance, all of them fading in comparison to this simple servant. Her cheekbones were well defined, her eyes tilted just slightly, enough to give her a faintly exotic look. Her skin was perfectly smooth, though tanned deeper than any girl Patience had ever known, and her figure, from what Patience could see under the loose gown, was perfect. She might have been a year or two Patience's senior, though she was much smaller than Patience herself. Suddenly feeling plainer that she ever had before, and realizing that she'd been staring at the girl, Patience looked down at the floor.

Ada hadn't seemed to notice. "You'd better climb in while the water is hot. It will stop the shivering, at least." She placed a piece of soap within easy reach of the tub. "I'm going to find you something better to wear."

She left the room and Patience barely hesitated before draping the cloak over a chair and stepping into the tub. She had never felt anything more wonderful in her life as she sat down, realizing that the tub was large enough that she could sit and be fully immersed in water up to her neck, while barely having to bend her knees. The tubs they had at home weren't nearly as roomy or comfortable, but still had to be carried by one of the manservants. Ada had managed this huge thing by herself, she must be very strong. Patience's mind wandered as she felt her body relax into the warmth. She considered the process of putting water into the tub and realized how much effort it would save people. In Patience's house, servants had to heat the water in a cauldron in the kitchen and bring it upstairs two bucketfuls at a time. By the time it reached the tub it had often cooled enough that Patience didn't wish to linger, but in this tub the water was almost too hot, and seemed to stay warm much longer than she was used to.

After her muscles relaxed enough that Patience didn't hurt anymore, she reached for the soap and the piece of flannel that Ada had left and applied herself to scrubbing off the accumulation of days. She had never been so dirty in her life. A few days of rough living and she looked like she had gone for a swim in the mud. The water turned black long before Patience was clean, but she did the best she could with her skin and her hair, ducking under the water to rinse the soap out. She longed for the fancy scented shampoo that had been a Christmas gift from her mother, but the soap wasn't harsh and seemed to do a relatively good job of cleaning.

As she emerged from a second dunking, Ada returned to the kitchen carrying a large piece of toweling and what looked like a white nightgown. She handed Patience the towel and looked away as Patience stood up, wrapped herself in the fabric and climbed out of the tub, wincing as her bare feet hit the cold floor. As she dried herself off, she watched Ada return the tube to the tub and attach the other end to yet a third pipe. Ada started cranking again and Patience blinked in amazement as the water disappeared through the tube in less than a minute. Ada returned the tub to the side room, hefting it easily, and returned just as Patience was ducking into the nightgown.

Ada used the cold water pipe to fill a kettle and placed it on a cast-iron stove to heat. While they waited for it to boil, she retrieved two cups and tossed a measure of tea leaves into a teapot. "Will you tell me how you came to be here?" Ada asked, uncertainly.

Patience, feeling relaxed and warm and full for the first time in days, let her true story spill out. She had meant to conceal certain details, but she was just too tired and comfortable to remember to. "It started with my engagement," she began. "I was engaged to Mr. Gabriel Longbranch of the Hammond and Company bank, the son of the head banker who is a superficial and supercilious ass," she stated definitively, then realized what had come out of her mouth and covered it with her hand in horror.

Ada looked like she was trying very hard to suppress a smile as she poured the tea and Patience, grateful she hadn't offended her hostess beyond hope of redemption, continued. "This engagement was without my consent and expressly against my wishes. The gentleman is close-minded and fully believes women should be seen and not heard to discuss anything except fashion or the weather. He does not approve of education for girls, or even literacy. He has stated on multiple occasions that reading will cause women to develop ideas not suited to our role in life and I certainly hope he is right, in that respect. I wanted desperately for an education, though my parents believed it was unnecessary for my future role as a wife and would not agree to anything more than deportment and music lessons. I have... had... have," Patience paused, unable to decide whether she should mention Mason and the uncertainty of his fate.

Finally she threw in an offhand mention, "My brother helped me to some schooling, hid me in his cupboard when his tutor was present, brought me books by the score, and distracted my parents so I could read them uninterrupted. My sisters together share the intellect of a donkey, and make that fact known far and wide. Both married well and I fear for their daughters. It is not my intention to marry at all, or certainly not to someone who shares my parents' archaic ideas. Women can do many things now, maybe even vote someday soon and I want to be in the middle of it all. I want to see the world and not be stuck in one city or town, traveling to London for the season and bearing children to a man who respects me a great deal less than his horses." She broke off the rant to look at Ada and was relieved to see only approval on the girl's face, not the censure she was half expecting.

"My engagement was announced publicly, I have a suspicion that I was the last person in our set to hear of it, and I left in haste, without properly preparing travel plans or suitable wardrobe." She continued on with her story, speaking of eating the unripe apples and sleeping in the ice house and barns, but left out mention of stealing from the house's garden. She very briefly glossed over the incident that had caused her to lose her few possessions, but saw sympathy and horror reflected by the girl. "So I was hiding in the woods, trying to decide where to go next when the storm came. I could not find shelter or relief from the rain that was pounding all sense from my head, so I climbed over the back wall and came in through an unlocked window. That's when you found me."

Ada looked at Patience levelly. "You said the creature saw you. What did you mean by that?" she looked nervous as she waited for the answer.

"I heard the great roaring coming from one of the rooms on the ground floor. I'm quite certain I was a bit out of my mind at that point, I was so cold and hungry that I followed the sound and peeked into the room where I saw it...him. What is it? I've never heard of anything like it really. Is it a Bigfoot?"

"A what?" Ada asked.

"It's a creature from the Americas. The Indians speak of a creature huge like a bear, but more man-shaped, who walks on legs like ours and has a face sort of like a big ape. But more intelligent. I read about it in a book once." Patience was proud of her knowledge and she hoped she had guessed right. It would make her more interesting to the other girl and maybe she'd want to let Patience stay if she proved she wasn't afraid of the beast.

Ada shook her head, looking confused. "I don't think so. At least, I don't know exactly what he is. Just that he has a terrible temper and tends to eat visitors. He mustn't know you are here. That's why you'll have to go in the morning." That last part sounded almost reluctant.

"But he did see me. At least, he looked right at me, and he did not hurt me. Unless he is blind? But then he should have been able to smell me, I think. I was in the room with him and he turned toward me and then just turned away again and roared out the window."

Inquisitiveness warred with nervousness on Ada's face and Patience wondered why.

"What else did he do?" Ada asked, though she seemed unsure if she wanted an answer.

"He just paced back and forth in front of the window. He roared a lot, it quite frightened me at first. That is all I saw him do. He seemed quite angry but he did not hurt me or chase me. Can he speak? Is he your master? What is it like working for a creature instead of a person?"

Despite her tiredness, Patience was too curious to let the chance for answers pass her by. She wanted to know about the creature, the same way she'd wanted to know about all the animals at the zoo when she was a child and had driven the zookeeper half-crazy as he tried to answer all her questions. Her mother had been very angry with her for pestering the man, and that was the last time she'd been taken on an outing of that type. After that they kept to parks and promenades and shopping, none of which interested Patience enough to bring up any questions.

Ada shook her head. "It's too hard to explain. It's very late now, you must be getting to sleep. Morning will come very soon."

As if on cue, Patience yawned widely. Embarrassed, she tried to conceal it but didn't do a very good job. Her exhaustion suddenly felt like it was weighing her down. She returned her empty teacup to the saucer-she hadn't even realized she'd finished her tea and stood up. The girl led her back up the stairs and opened a door that had previously been closed. It led to a smallish room that was very neat and tidy. The bed was freshly made with crisp sheets and a thick quilt to keep out the chill.

Patience's bare feet stepped onto a thick rug with relief. It was too cold to be wandering the house without shoes and she wondered what she'd been thinking, except that she hadn't been offered slippers, and she didn't know where her boots were anyway. She suddenly remembered that she'd made a mess, dripping all over the hallway and on her visit to the library, and felt ashamed at making extra work for Ada. No wonder the girl wanted her gone. She started to apologize but Ada cut her off.

"It doesn't matter. It's just water, and it can be quickly taken care of in the morning. Now, climb under the covers before you take any more of a chill and I'll be back to fetch you in the morning."

Yawning again, Patience did as instructed, relishing the warmth of the fabric over her. A small fire had been laid in the grate and it kept the worst of the cold away from the small room. She smiled at Ada. "Thank you. Likely you saved my life tonight. If I had taken sick I would have had no chance at all."

Ada waved away the suggestion. "I understand about not having choices or chances. Don't worry about it. I'll see you in the morning." She handed Patience the lamp she carried and turned around, closing the bedroom door behind her.

Patience placed the lamp on the bedside table and turned it down to the very faintest glow. She closed her eyes and was asleep almost before her head hit the pillow.

CHAPTER SEVEN

PATIENCE HAD just opened her eyes upon a room full of light when a knock sounded at her door.

"Come in," she called, sitting up and stretching luxuriously under the covers.

She felt no shame being seen in her nightgown, this was generally how her morning started, and she was surprised when Ada entered the room keeping her eyes averted from Patience and the bed. Ada carried a tray crammed with different breakfast foods. There were eggs cooked at least three ways, sausages and some sort of roast meat, potatoes and tomatoes and bread with little pots of something to spread on them. There were several kinds of greens and a few things Patience didn't recognize at all. Her eyes widened at the amount of food. She quickly moved the lamp away from the bedside table to make room for the laden tray. Her home life provided opulent breakfasts on a daily basis, but since she'd left, the scarcity of food had become a regular occurrence and the idea of all this food just for her seemed suddenly strange and foreign.

Ada plopped the tray down and removed a basket that Patience hadn't noticed from the crook of her arm, placing it on the floor beside the table. From her other arm she draped Patience's dress and underthings onto the bed and dropped her boots beside it. Patience stared at the boots, suddenly remembering what she'd left out of her story the night before.

Ada nodded. "I know you were here before last night. And I found your boots around the side of the house where you dropped them." She said this forthrightly.

Patience blushed. "I did not think you would let me stay if you knew I was stealing from your garden. I was just so hungry and I did not know where to find food. I deeply apologize and if there is ever anything I can do to make it up to you, I will."

Ada shrugged. "It really doesn't matter. There's lots of food in the garden. That's why I didn't say anything. You've only come a few times, and I watched to make sure you weren't taking more than I could spare. It's not your fault you were hungry, not really."

Patience lowered her eyes to the tray and then looked back up at Ada. "It looks as if I might never be hungry again, should I consume all of this. Please tell me this is not all for me."

Ada shrugged again. "I don't know what you like

to eat for breakfast, so I brought you a few options."

"A few options that might feed an army barracks," Patience teased, lifting the tray onto the bed so she could reach it and noting that the other girl smiled in response. Patience was relieved that Ada wasn't angry about the stealing. "Do take a seat and help me manage this breakfast." She drew her legs up and shifted over in the bed, patting the mattress beside her in invitation for Ada to join her.

Ada eyed the space and blushed. Patience noted that she even did that prettily, a pale rose flush in her cheeks, not at all splotchy or dark. She knew she wouldn't have managed to look so well if she were as embarrassed as Ada seemed.

"I couldn't. Really. I made the food for you," Ada insisted.

"And you made a grand amount of food, so unless you want it wasted, you have no choice. Unless you want to invite the beast up to partake?" Patience clamped her mouth shut, suddenly afraid Ada might do just that. She really did not want to share a meal with a creature as likely to eat her as the eggs and toast.

Ada shook her head forcefully. "No! He mustn't know you are here." She reluctantly took the space on the bed, after searching the room with her eyes and discovering a lack of chairs or other seating possibilities.

Patience was amused again. How strange this girl was. So proper in some respects and strangely free in others. She had certainly never met a servant girl who acted anything like Ada, nor any of her own set. She thought she might be able to make friends with this stranger, something that she'd never really managed with the girls she knew at home, even her own sisters. She wondered if Ada could read, or if she liked to. It would be so nice to discuss books with someone again. She hadn't had the chance since Mason left. She almost posed the question, but how did one tactfully ask if another person could read? Shaking her head she applied herself to spreading what looked like raspberry jam onto a piece of toast.

As there was no second set of cutlery, Ada picked up a roasted tomato in her fingers, cupping her other hand below in case a seed dropped. "Oh!" she suddenly exclaimed, shoving the fruit whole into her mouth and freeing her hands to reach down to the basket. She pulled out the copy of David Copperfield that Patience had been reading when she fell asleep in the library. "I thought you might want to finish the story," she mumbled around her mouthful.

Patience wiped her hands carefully on the linen napkin that had been tucked under one of the plates before taking the book from the other girl. "Does that mean I can stay?" she asked hopefully.

"Oh no. I mean, you couldn't. But I thought you could take it with you. There are so many books here, many more than I could ever read. And it would keep you company, I thought." Ada blushed again, her words tumbling over each other.

Patience's heart sank but she bit back her disappointment. "Have you read it? David Copperfield I mean?" That was much more polite than asking if Ada could read, she thought with satisfaction.

Ada nodded. "Several times. It was one of my father's favorites and he gave it to me before I turned ten."

If Ada had been encouraged to read by her father, it was a vast divergence from Patience's upbringing. She wondered how different her life would have been with a parent who had more interest in a daughter's mind.

Ada was still talking. "He always brought home Dickens, really he brought home every book he could get his hands on. He would read them and then give them to me, so we would have things to talk about. When I was very young he would read the stories to me, nearly every night before bed. And sometimes he would forget himself and would read all night, even if I fell asleep. I'd wake up and he'd still be reading out loud as if I hadn't missed a word."

She giggled, but then stopped and looked sad.

"Do you still see him?" Patience asked.

Ada's eyes filled with tears. "He went away, on a journey, and he hasn't come back. I don't have any idea where he's gone," she swallowed heavily, "but sometimes he's so absentminded, he will head off somewhere and get completely turned around and interested in something new. Once he went away for four months and hadn't realized he'd been gone more than a few weeks. When I was young I'd be sent off to London to stay with my mother's sister Agatha. She was like your parents, I think," Ada ventured. "She wanted me to be a 'proper young lady' and never say anything and dress perfectly and wear a corset, even before I was twelve. I hated it there," she confided in Patience. "I always begged my father to take me with him. And sometimes he did for shorter trips. And when I was thirteen I simply refused to be sent to London, so I stayed at home. Of course, there were other people there, but no one much minded what I did so I could read all day or built a fort out of pillows or walk through the woods for hours and no one was bothered."

"Not even your mother?" Patience asked. She was never left alone for five minutes to do as she liked. She could barely imagine whole days of it, or at least she couldn't have before she ran away.

Ada shrugged again. She seemed to do that a lot. Patience tried it, another thing she would have been castigated for at home. "My mother died before that. She was sick for a while, too, but I know she loved me. She would read to me too, or tell me stories that she made up in her head. I don't remember much about it but my father always reminds me of everything about her. So I won't forget. I wish I had a daguerreotype. I don't remember very well what she looked like, though father says I look just like her, so maybe I can see her if I look in the mirror long enough. I try it sometimes, but I haven't found her yet."

"So how did you come to be here?" Patience asked.

Ada's face closed off. "I've been here a while," she stated, clearly intending not to discuss it further. Patience thought she could imagine the story. A lone girl whose father disappeared, and with no resources.

What else could she do but go into service? She might have tried for a governess' position, but she was young, lacked references, and her manners were too relaxed to find a place in a good home. Patience was in a similar position and she hoped Ada's kindred situation could help her.

She applied herself to the breakfast and didn't ask any more questions for a while, as she sliced up eggs and toast and sausage, encouraging Ada to eat as well. The roasted meat tasted a bit like rabbit, and she wondered where it had come from. She decided that might be a neutral enough question to get the conversation back on track.

"Where did you get the rabbit?" she queried. "I saw lots of vegetables and some fruit trees in the garden, but no rabbit hutches." She looked at Ada to see if she'd answer.

"I made a trap. Several in fact. No matter about the high walls, animals do seem to make their way into the garden and some of them make lovely dinners. I have chickens though, around the side. That's where the eggs come from. I'm surprised you didn't hear them clucking, they usually do in the mornings."

Patience stood up and went to the window, pushing aside the thin sheers that still covered the glass. She looked down and saw the back garden, and no chickens, but when she listened for them she could hear a faint clucking. "How clever. Our cook kept a few chickens, but would usually get frustrated when they hid their eggs and would turn them into dinner themselves sooner or later."

She returned to the bed, holding onto the tray so nothing would spill as she slid back under the covers. The fire had gone out at some point and the air was a bit chilly. There was no sign of rain though, and if she did have to leave at least she wouldn't be soaked immediately. She really didn't want to leave and was trying to think of a way to make that clear.

Ada was still talking about food. "Sometimes I can shoot down birds that fly overhead. My father taught me to use a bow, but I'm not very accurate. I don't suppose you know how to shoot?"

"Certainly not!" Patience confirmed. "My mother would have fallen into a faint at the idea. 'That would be highly unladylike'," she stated, aping her mother's flawless diction and tone. "'A young lady has no need to learn the gentlemanly pursuits, except to smile and fawn over his accomplishments, should he have any.' I think she would have preferred for me not to learn anything since walking and talking. Likely not even talking, if possible."

Ada giggled again, finding comedy in what, to Patience, was just reality. It encouraged her to continue. "And my father! 'No young woman of my acquaintance has ever suggested such a ridiculous concept. Learning to shoot? You might as well take up fan dancing and hire yourself out as a circus acrobat!' He commented on the circus acrobat a lot. To the point where it was my greatest aspiration when I was about ten. If he could think of nothing more degrading for me to be, it would have to be a lot more fun than what he did want."

Now Ada was laughing so hard she was shaking.

"Can you do any acrobatics?" she asked, when she had calmed down enough to speak.

"Not a one, unless you count hanging upside down from a tree limb by my knees. Mason taught me to do that when I was four or five. One day I was practicing, hanging from a tree in the back garden, my hair touching the ground and my dress fallen over my face when I heard my mother gasp so loudly it startled me and I tumbled to the ground. When I had sorted myself out and realized who it was, I thought my life expectancy might resemble that of the hen I had already seen killed that morning for supper. I never got to taste the hen though, as I was sent to my room without so much as a crust of bread for the next few days.

"Mason snuck me in some fruit and cheese. He felt responsible for teaching me, and not ensuring our parents were elsewhere. He tried to explain that to Mother, but she wouldn't hear of it. It was all right for Mason to do wrong, he was a boy and our father's heir, so some mistakes could be overlooked, but for a 'young lady' to be showing everything from the neck down by hanging from the trees? A scandal! What if someone had seen me? My marriage prospects would have been ruined! Never mind that I was barely out of diapers at the time. Everything I did, she believed, would ruin my chance for a good marriage. You know, I never once heard her speak of a happy marriage. I wonder if those exist too."

Ada nodded. "Of course they do. I've seen many happy marriages. My parents were happy, I'm sure of it, until my mother died. And my father never wanted to remarry. He said no one could be like my mother, so there was no point. And our cook when I was little was married for nearly thirty years to the same man, and loved visiting her children and grandchildren on her days off. Her husband was a footman nearby so they could see each other over the wall when he drove past and they always smiled at each other. She retired a long time ago, and they went to live with their oldest daughter's family somewhere in the North. But it seemed like a perfect fairy tale to me, even with no prince."

"I met a prince once," Patience mentioned. "He was fat and sweaty and very self-important. That pretty much ruined fairy tales for me."

Ada laughed again.

Patience noticed the way her eyes sparkled and there was a dimple on her left cheek, but none on her right. Patience thought how lovely that was. She didn't have dimples, they had always seemed to belong to a different sort of girl, and she suspected her eyes never sparkled like that either. Truthfully, she rarely laughed that freely. She let herself laugh now, more in delight at the chance to do so with another girl than because she thought anything she'd said was that humorous. It was a freeing feeling. She wished she had someone to laugh with all the time.

Patience watched Ada surreptitiously, pretending to look for something else to eat on the tray, which they had managed to demolish thoroughly. She longed to bring up the topic of staying again, but didn't know how to go about it. She wanted to stay more than ever, not just because of the warmth and the food, but because it had been so long since she had laughed at all, or had someone to really talk to without having to censor every word. She fell silent and Ada looked at her, again, blushing slightly.

"I suppose I had better get dressed," Patience said, nodding to her dress at the bottom of the bed.

Ada was dressed similarly to how she had been the night before, and Patience was beginning to feel odd about still being in a nightdress, especially one that wasn't hers.

Ada slid off the bed, placing the tray back on the table where it had started. She lifted the basket up to replace it and uncovered the contents. It mostly held food: what looked like a cold roasted chicken, fruit and vegetables, a couple of loafs of bread and some nuts. Traveling food.

Patience could also see a comb and brush and a small mirror, some soap, a sewing case and warm stockings, things that she should have had with her from the start had her trip been better planned.

"You can take the cloak too, the one you wore last night, and the book of course," Ada said, sounding slightly reluctant. "Please tell me if there's anything else you need. I wasn't sure..."

Patience felt her heart heave miserably within her. She stared at the basket and unbidden, tears rose to her eyes. She bit her lip to keep them from falling. "Please do not make me leave," she whispered without looking up.

She heard only silence. She raised her eyes to Ada's face and saw that the dark-haired girl had gone pale. She didn't immediately deny Patience's request this time, though, so the pleading continued. "I do not believe I can continue. I know nothing about traveling without servants and chests and train tickets. I am scared all the time. I was so hungry and so cold and it is just going to get worse. I never thought about what I would do once I left home, just that I had to leave. I have never been so stupid in my life. But I know I could help you here. I saw no other servants, and you cannot look after this whole house on your own. I could tidy and sweep and polish. I could cook or scour the pots or anything else you need help with. I know I do not know everything, but I am a quick learner and I promise you would only have to show me once."

She took a breath and then continued immediately, as if by leaving a pause she would be inviting Ada to refuse her. "I know you are strong and clever but it is such a big house and I would not need wages at all, just a little food. I could work in your garden and collect eggs from your chickens and learn to butcher the animals you trap. I will do anything you want. And when your masters get home I will beg them to keep me on. I promise I will not get you into trouble. Just please do not send me away. I never had a friend before." Patience's head was empty of more words that might help convince Ada but she was terrified to look up at the girl and see the denial that she knew was coming.

When there was no immediate response, Patience risked a quick glance. Ada wasn't looked at her, wasn't seemingly looking at anything. She was chewing on her lip and looked very deep in thought.

Patience wouldn't risk interrupting for anything, as long as it ended in her favor. She waited possibly the longest couple of minutes of her life before Ada spoke.

"If you promised to only stay on this floor, and not to go downstairs ever, the creature doesn't come up here. And if you stayed pretty quiet, no one but me would know you were here. Maybe it wouldn't hurt to try it for a while. But you'd have to promise to stay on this floor. There's nothing upstairs, just a lot of rooms that aren't used anymore so they are closed up. But you must promise not to go up there and not to go downstairs ever. If the creature sees you there, he will eat you. But you could go in all the rooms on this floor and read the books. And then we could talk about them, if you wanted to. Can you promise me that? To just stay here and not go off exploring?"

Patience nodded so fast her neck hurt. "I will promise anything you want. And I will do all the cleaning on this floor, so you will not have to worry about it. If you show me where the rags and brooms are kept I can start now. Anything!"

Ada smiled, though more faintly than before. "You should probably get dressed first. You don't have to worry about that, I take care of everything. Just stay in these rooms. And I tried to mend your dress but I'm afraid it's beyond my skill. There are clothes hanging in some of the cupboards in the other bedrooms. Feel free to wear anything you can fit into. I need to take these things downstairs now, but I'll come back later to visit. I hope you won't be too bored." She went to pick up the tray but Patience forestalled her by pulling her into a hug.

Ada responded "oh" in surprise as Patience squeezed her gently. Patience wasn't actually sure who she had surprised more. She hadn't meant to hug the girl, just to thank her. Patience had never hugged anyone who wasn't related to her, and hadn't hugged anyone at all since the day her brother left for training. Startled, she released Ada and stepped back, her face flaming. She did not blush prettily so she turned to look out the window as Ada gathered the tray and the basket and took them out of the room. Patience heard her feet going down the stairs as she wondered whatever had possessed her.

CHAPTER EIGHT

IT WAS a wonderful treat to be able to lie around in a warm, safe bed, to be fed and properly dressed and to be able to read any book at any time Patience wanted without having to hide. Even more thrilling was the chance to talk about the books with an interested and informed person. While Mason had been a help in giving books to Patience to read, he hadn't usually read them himself and wasn't interested in discussing them.

Ada had seemingly read every book in the library and had things to say about each of them. They talked about character flaws and plot points and the difference between male and female authors. Even which characters they would want to be. But Patience could only talk books and let's pretend while Ada was free, and she seemed to have a lot of things to do for most of the day.

"But why can I not help?" Patience asked. "To be fair I have never exactly cleaned before, but I am sure sweeping and mopping a floor cannot be as difficult as all that," she insisted to Ada one morning over breakfast taken in Patience's room. Ada had introduced a table and chairs into the corner and it was much easier to eat when sitting properly in a chair than tucked into a bed.

"I just don't need help," Ada insisted, as she had before. "Taking care of the house doesn't take that much time, really. I have a system all worked out."

"I would like to be useful," Patience commented, as she had on similar occasions over the last week or so. "Surely there must be something." When she really thought about it though, she never saw any dust or dirt in any of the rooms she explored. Even the ones that didn't seem to be in use. She just didn't know how it was possible. She never saw Ada in the library or her bedroom with a dusting rag, but even under the bed (Patience had peeked) there was not the faintest sign of dust bunnies.

Ada thought about it. "I suppose you could polish the silverware. I can bring it up to you after we eat."

Patience nodded eagerly. At least she would feel useful for a few minutes. The butler usually polished the silverware in her home. It was considered an important task, making sure the valuable pieces looked perfect, and not ever left to a lesser servant. But her heart sank when Ada brought the pieces upstairs. To her they already looked polished, and clearly this was just make-work. Still, she listened carefully as Ada explained.

"The larger pieces go in the bucket, and the smaller in the bowl. You pour this solution into each, up to where the black mark is," she pointed to a clearly drawn line in the bucket that was about an inch long, "then you drop the silver in and count to 60 seconds, pull them out using the tongs, and drop them in the water here." She indicated a large basin full of warm water. "Try not to let the solution touch your skin, it'll sting, and it can burn if you don't wash it off quickly."

Patience was confused. "At home the butler spends hours polishing with silver polish. When does that part come in?" Ada hadn't brought any polish, that she could see, and no rags to wipe anything off.

Ada smiled. "We don't use that here. This is much easier. My father created the solution, one of his successes. It only takes 60 seconds, once a month, and the silver looks perfect. Probably it could go longer between cleanings, but that was what he recommended. The solution removes any tarnish that has built up on the silver and seals it so no oxygen can get in to create further tarnishing. My father worked this process out in order to save servants all that effort just to keep silver looking nice.

"Your butler probably spent hours each week doing what we can do here in a single minute. And as it's only done once a month, and anyone can do it, the servant could be used for more interesting or necessary labor. Father has created many labor-saving devices, like this. He means to patent them and release them for widespread use." She had seemed happy when describing the use of the product but now her face fell. "I mean, he will when he returns. I could do so on his behalf, but that would indicate to people that he's unavailable." She shook her head as if to clear her mind. "Anyway, I'll leave you to the chore. I have some stew on the stove and I want to make sure it doesn't scorch."

She left Patience alone with the silver, the solution, and her thoughts. She was very curious about Ada's father. He seemed to be a man of some great intellect but also strange. He had encouraged his daughter's mind and education, which was unlike any father Patience had ever run across, but he had also left her alone to fend for herself. Ada seemed to believe he was coming back some day, but he had clearly been gone long enough that she had had to take a domestic position in order to keep herself fed and housed. This led to wondering about the owners of the home she presently occupied. Ada had not spoken of them except to allude to some form of travel.

And why would they leave a sole servant girl in charge of a large house and a horrid monster? Had the creature arrived after they left? If so, how was Ada keeping it controlled? She made Patience stay upstairs in order to avoid the creature knowing she was there, but didn't seem at all worried that it would scent her, or hear her and climb the stairs itself. Was the creature intelligent? Patience had seen no sign of gates or barriers keeping it from climbing to the first floor, but it never had. She heard the roaring sometimes, and stayed in her room with the door closed when she did, but the sound never varied and seemed to take place only in one or two rooms, both facing the front of the house. It didn't seem to care for the back rooms.

And why were the drapes drawn so close everywhere the creature was not. Ada had made her promise not to open the drapes in the front of the house, though she was free to look out over the back garden all she wanted. The whole thing made no sense. She shook her head. *Best get to work,* she thought, with no little amusement.

She poured the solution into the two containers, stopping exactly at the black indicators. Then she dropped each piece of silver in, as many as would fit, counted to 60 and removed the pieces to place them in the water. When she carefully examined a fork, she could see no difference before and after its bath, but she shrugged and continued. The whole tray of silver that Ada had brought her took less than five minutes and then her task was done. That wasn't really what she'd meant when she asked for something to do.

She didn't want to call down to Ada to say she was done, in case the beast heard her, so she left the containers where they were on the table and walked over to the window. It was a cold and gloomy day. No sun peeked through heavy clouds and she was sure it would start raining in the next little while. She shuddered, remembering the chill she'd taken when she'd been caught by the storm earlier in the month. She hoped she was never that cold again. Even the memory of it chilled her down to her toes. She gazed around for something to do, found nothing as usual, and picked up a book, pulling one of the chairs nearer the fire so she could warm her feet as she read.

Patience was beginning to feel like a caged animal. She paced up and down the hallway, counting her steps. She knew this corridor intimately, could have walked it blindfolded and told a listener exactly what she was passing at any given moment. For variety she went into each room as she passed and looked outside, careful not to dislodge the curtains over the windows that faced the front. The sun shone but she could see a rime of frost in a few places. She gazed over the back garden, wishing she could at least visit that. She made up her mind to ask Ada about it when the girl brought up lunch. Surely if she was quiet the creature would not be roused by a single girl taking the stairs and going directly outside, especially if she walked with Ada so any sound could be attributed to her.

Below, Ada entered the garden from the back door, armed with a bucket and spade. Clearly she was intending to weed the garden. Although Patience had never been much interested in growing things, since her experience in the woods she'd developed a fascination with recognizing edibles. She'd found a book on different kinds of plant growth and was working at memorizing everything that grew in the British climate, just in case. For a while she watched Ada crouch among the neat rows of plants, digging carefully and depositing greens in her bucket. Finally, it gave Patience an idea. If Ada was likely to be occupied for a while, then Patience could do a bit more exploring. She didn't dare descend the stairs, she had promised multiple times not to, but the upper floors had only been mentioned in passing. Ada said most of the rooms were closed up, and there was nothing of interest up there, but at this point Patience would be interested in just about anything new. She listened carefully for any sounds coming from downstairs, and checked again to make sure Ada was still working intently, then slowly and carefully climbed the narrower set of stairs leading to the second floor.

At the top, her stomach churning with nervousness, Patience nearly turned back. The last thing she wanted was to make Ada angry with her. Ada was the one who provided food and shelter and friendship and Patience could afford to scorn none of those things. But she threw her shoulders back and convinced herself that she would just take a quick look around and then return to her room as if nothing had happened.

She peeked into the first room. White cloths covered all the furniture, giving it a slightly sinister look. She expected the floors to be dusty, and to have to watch where she stepped so she didn't leave tracks, but there wasn't a bit of dust anywhere she could see. She lifted up one cloth to reveal a round card table marked out for some game, and a second revealed a billiards table. Clearly Ada's employers didn't spend much time in the games room. The next room held a large bed, made up with a thick duvet, and a door off that led to a ladies' dressing area. A cupboard held women's clothing, all several years out of fashion, making Patience wonder about who had inhabited the room. Had the owners of the house been gone long enough for fashions to have changed so completely? That wasn't possible, because Ada couldn't have been there that long. This trip was doing nothing but confusing Patience, and she almost returned downstairs.

She hesitated in the corridor, her head swiveling towards the stairs and then away again. She decided to check out one more room at random. Closing her eyes, she spun around and pointed, a popular way of making a decision when she was small, and when she opened her eyes again she followed her finger to the room at the very furthest end of the hall. The door was closed firmly, like all the others, but was not locked. Patience expected yet another bedroom or sitting room but the open door revealed something quite different.

Counters lined all four walls, breaking only for the doorway. She wasn't sure what they were made of, something that definitely wasn't wood. She touched it, and felt a hard but smooth surface, mottled in color. It didn't feel like stone or tile or anything she would have expected, it was too smooth. But that didn't hold her attention for long because what the counters held was much more interesting.

On one wall there were all kinds of jars and bowls and containers of different colored liquids, lined up at the back of the counters to create work space in front. Shelves above held more jars, some of them in colors she'd never seen before, not even in the paintings of the museums she had attended. A second counter was covered with hundreds or thousands of pieces of metal in varying shapes and sizes. Tools and parts hung neatly from the wall above that counter, some simple ones that she recognized from home, but many were more elaborate and she couldn't imagine their uses.

She recognized the tiny cogs and wheels and springs from an accident Mason had once had with a clock. Well, he had said it was an accident, anyway. Patience had had her suspicions he had just wanted to see what made it go. But her father had spanked him and sent him to his room for three days. It was one of the few occasions that Patience had had to sneak food to her brother, instead of the other way around. He still wouldn't admit to having done it on purpose, even to her.

How he would have loved to see this place!

Pushing her sadness aside, Patience went to the longest counter, the one that ran under the window. As it faced the back of the house, the curtain was not fully drawn and bright light filtered into the room through it. She stared in amazement. There were all manner of creations. Some she recognized as toys, things she had seen in toy-shops as a child, or even in her own home. She picked up a baby doll that cried when it was lifted upright and whose eyes closed when it was laid down. She'd had a similar doll when she was young, although this one seemed much more realistic. The face was not china, but she wasn't sure what it was. Some kind of leather possibly, it resembled human skin too closely for her comfort. With a slight shudder she replaced it exactly where it had been.

Then her eyes fell on a cat. For a minute she was sure it was real, and she wondered why she hadn't seen it before, but it didn't move, even when she cautiously stroked its back. Another toy. She picked it up and turned it over. A tiny key poked up from its belly. Patience had seen clockwork toys before. There had even been an automaton boy who could write his name at an exhibit the last time she had been in London, so she turned the key a few times to see what the cat would do. When it stretched out its paws she put it back on the table and watched in amazement as it started to clean itself. Then it got up and walked over to the edge of the counter, and then turned around again and mewed in her direction. It paced back to where it started and turned around a few times, tail swishing, until it seemed to find a comfortable position. Patience reached out to stroke its fur again and the thing purred. How extraordinary. If she hadn't seen the key she would never have been able to tell that it wasn't a real cat. It seemed to go to sleep and she moved on to another item.

Patience was so absorbed by the trinkets and toys she found that she forgot where she was, and forgot that she had meant to return to her room after only a few minutes. She turned keys and watched a dozen or more creations go through their paces, always real enough to fool an onlooker. Some were clockwork and others seemed to have systems powered by things she had no idea about, but the operation of them all were simple and she considered what uses they had.

She was right in the middle of examining a round creation that seemed to suck air in through vents on the bottom, though she wasn't sure for what purpose, when she heard an indrawn breath behind her.

She spun around to face Ada, who wore a look of utter betrayal. Patience's heart missed a beat. She'd known that Ada would be angry if she found out Patience had been exploring, but this didn't look like anger to her. Beyond the betrayal seemed to be stark terror.

"Ada, I..." she broke off, really having nothing to say to explain her behavior.

"Go." Ada said, quietly. "You need to leave."

Patience walked past and out into the hallway. She preceded the other girl down the stairs and started to enter her room.

"No," Ada stated, starting to sound agitated. "You need to get out. Go. Don't come back."

Patience stood stock still and stared at the girl. "Leave the house?" she asked, tears springing to her eyes.

Ada's own eyes were already filled. "You have to leave now! Take the cloak and get out. I told you. I told you that you could stay as long as you stayed on this floor but you didn't... you went... you have to leave!" at the last word her voice rose until she was shouting at Patience. "Go away! I don't want you here anymore."

Patience took a step towards her, her arms outstretched. "Ada, please, I did not mean to..."

"GO!"

The last word was a command she couldn't

contradict. Patience fled down the stairs, grabbed a cloak from the hook beside the back door, climbed the wall where she'd gotten into the garden on her first visit and fled into the woods, tears streaming down her face. She ran until she couldn't breathe and then sank to the ground, gasping for air and pulling at the cloak to cover every part of her. Then she curled into a ball and wept.

CHAPTER NINE

ALTHOUGH IT hurt her heart terribly to see the house where she'd been happy for such a short time, the pain was worse when she wasn't near enough to feel its presence. Patience scouted out the area around the house until she knew it as well as the floor of the interior she'd spent so many days exploring. The woods were close enough to the house's wall that if Patience climbed a tall tree she could see over into the garden. From this perch she watched Ada enter and leave the house, tend the garden, feed the chickens and kill and skin the small animals that got caught in her snares.

Sometimes she told herself it was wrong to watch without Ada knowing she was there, but she felt magnetically drawn there day after day. She also discovered a small village nearby. Although she didn't enter the village, for reasons she never tried to explain to herself, she could see some of it from the edge of the woods where she felt safe. She noted a market day once, where people came to buy and sell goods from temporary tables made out of rough-hewn planks or from blankets laid on the ground.

It was cold in the woods, and even with the warm cloak, she still spent more time than not shivering. Once she tried to build a fire, she'd read that there was a way to make a spark by rubbing two sticks together but it certainly didn't work for her. She wished she'd taken some matches when she'd fled. She'd grown used to being warm in the house. Constant chill just added misery to her loneliness. In truth, she missed Ada's companionship more than the warmth or the food, which was why she kept close to the house where she was no longer welcome.

At least she wasn't having as much trouble finding food now, thanks to her study of the horticulture book from the library. She knew what was safe to eat and even in this late season there was food around, though it wasn't terribly appetizing. She ate only when the hunger pangs reminded her to, but they didn't come that frequently.

She did tend to fall into weeping fits for no particular reason and she knew she felt lonelier than she ever had before, even lonelier than when she'd first run away. Feeling close to someone, even for a short time, had been so new and wonderful that Patience despaired when she thought she might never find it again.

She wondered if women got married simply to stop the lonely feelings. Even a husband one did not love would be someone to talk to, to share space with. She started to feel like maybe it wouldn't be so bad to be married after all, just not to Gabriel. She knew that a marriage such as that would leave her lonelier than ever, even if the man was right beside her. To him she would not be someone to converse with or share ideas, her role would be more like that of a dress or a piece of her mother's jewelry, something to show off for a while and then put away in a cupboard or a box until it was needed again. Even being lonely and cold and miserable in the middle of a forest somewhere (she still had no idea where she was, she'd never gotten around to asking Ada) was better than that.

At least here she was a person.

She was sitting on her favorite perch in her favorite tree, watching the dark clouds build up worryingly when she heard the beast roaring from the front of the house. With nothing else to lose she decided she would have a good look at him and see if she could figure out exactly what he was. She circled the house, staying as close to the woods as possible until she found a place she could view him clearly, but was still out of his sight. She watched him pace up and down in front of the window a few times, then stand and roar, and then return to pacing. He repeated these actions several times and then the curtains closed him from her view.

Patience stayed where she was. Something was ticking in her brain and she needed to think. Because of this, she was still in position when the front door opened and the creature stood framed in the opening, roaring again. Then he left the door for a few seconds and returned, back and forth. He looked like he was pacing, exactly as he'd done at the window, but it wasn't as visible because the door was a narrower opening. He stopped to roar again and then was gone.

She realized that the creature only exhibited a very few actions. He walked, but each time he paced, the distance covered seemed about the same, whether in front of the door or the window. He would stop and roar, but each time it sounded the same, and seemed to go on for the same amount of time. And he would stand still and move his head, seeming to look around him, but when he had looked right at her in the house, he hadn't reacted as if he actually saw her.

These actions never changed. Patience knew from recent experience that pacing back and forth in one place got very boring very quickly. She had learned to alter her steps, to go into and out of rooms, and to change her paces to keep herself from going crazy. If the creature was a thinking being, he would be bound to do the same. And if he was a wild animal, he would not be confined by those same actions. He would likely have eaten Ada and whatever else he could find in the house and then gone looking for another food source.

Patience's mind proffered the image of a cat that looked real but was wound like clockwork to perform a set of actions. She remembered the way it had walked across the desk and then curled itself up. She had only wound it once, but strongly believed that if she was back up in that room and wound it again, it would perform the same activities in the same order.

It was like that with the automaton she'd seen in London. It could write its name, but that was all. It dipped the pen in ink, brought it to paper and wrote the same characters, over and over. If, as had happened while she was watching, the paper was not placed correctly, it would write on the desk below. Everyone had laughed at that, and she had drifted off to see another exhibit, but that memory was strong right now.

The creature must be another toy. Something that needed to be wound up and placed carefully in order to perform. She didn't understand why anyone would create such a thing. The cat was cute and would be an interesting item to discuss at a dinner party. The other toys she'd seen upstairs had been for entertainment mostly, or else they did something useful, but what use could a great, scary creature have? She supposed it might frighten away burglars, should any happen to approach the house when the creature was roaring, but then wouldn't it make sense to set it up at night, when thieves were more likely to arrive?

Patience had never heard the roaring at night except for the night she arrived, only in the daytime when Ada was up and about. But never, she realized, when Ada was with her. The creature only seemed to come out when Ada was on the ground floor, and not when she was in the garden either. That would make sense if Ada was the one winding it up and setting it off, but for what purpose? What possible use could a creature like that have except to scare people?

And it would, she realized. In the time she'd spent in the house, no one had ever approached it. No doorbell sound or knocking had come at the front door, and she'd never heard a delivery boy or caller of any kind. Was that the creature's purpose? To keep everyone away? It hadn't worked in her case, but she'd been desperate enough that a quick death at the claws or jaws of the creature had seemed preferable to freezing in the storm. What if no one else was that despairing? No friendly housewife or visiting clergy was likely to want to broach that great a threat just to say hello.

As far as Patience was aware, Ada never went out the front door. She only used the back, into the view-restricted garden where no one could see in unless they were up a tree. But again, that was something that Patience had started out of loneliness and despair. She already believed the creature wouldn't hurt her, especially not with her outside the walls. But a visitor would not be likely to want to see into a space occupied by a frightening creature. As far as anyone in the village was aware, no person inhabited the house. Suddenly the restriction on moving the drapes from the front windows made perfect sense. Ada didn't want anyone to know she was there. She wanted them to think the beast was the only resident of the home so they would leave her alone.

But why? Did the owners of the house demand this of Ada while they were away? Was it for her protection or theirs? Were there actually employers?

Patience suddenly put everything together. Ada wasn't a servant in the house, her plain clothes and relaxed manners had just made Patience believe that was the girl's position, because in Patience's experience, Ada hadn't exhibited the training or the formality expected from a well-off daughter.

But Ada had herself said that her father hadn't cared if she acted like a young lady or not. He encouraged her to read and think about the things she read. He probably hadn't much cared about what she wore or whether she observed the proper formalities. And he was an inventor, a creator. All the things in the upstairs workshop were his creations. Just like the tarnish-repelling solution she had cleaned the silver with.

She suddenly felt terrible for treating Ada so poorly when the girl had been nothing but kind to her. Clearly, she hadn't wanted anyone to know she lived in the house, but she let Patience stay there, despite the fact that she didn't know the truth. Her father had left her alone and not returned, causing the girl to fend entirely for herself. And she must not have had anywhere to go. She was managing to feed herself and do the cooking and cleaning without any kind of assistance. Yet there had been flour for bread and sugar and tea and things that couldn't be grown in the garden. So something must be coming in from outside, unless her supply store was enormous. She wondered exactly how long Ada had been alone.

Patience was still staring at the closed front door where the beast had departed. How incredibly brave and clever the girl must be, to decide to stay there unaided and to find a way to keep everyone else from bothering her. She moved deeper into the woods, and circled around the back of the house again, musing on whether Ada's father had built the creature or whether Ada had managed it by herself. Certainly the things on the table didn't seem to have been abandoned for long. She must still be working up there, with her father away. Patience wondered what else she had created. The questions burgeoned in her mind one after the other. It was impossible to know the truth. Everything in her mind was just speculation. She couldn't stay away now. She had to know everything.

CHAPTER TEN

INTENDING TO confront Ada, Patience was halfway over the wall before she thought about Ada's possible reaction. She'd been so angry when Patience had broken her word, but was it the broken promise that had hurt her or fear of her deception being discovered? Patience wasn't sure how best to approach the subject, but she would have to tell Ada what she thought or she would spend her whole life wondering. And she wasn't sure what kind of life it could be.

At least with Ada she felt safe, and it was more than the food and the roof over her head. She'd never felt particularly safe in her own home, always having to watch every word, every gesture, to make sure she wasn't disappointing her parents or defying their expectations. But with Ada it was different. She could say what was in her heart. She wasn't willing to let that feeling go so soon after finding it.

Realizing she'd been sitting on the wall for far too long, and knowing that if Ada saw her there was a possibility that she'd lock the house up to keep her out, Patience quickly let herself down into the garden and strode to the back door. It was unlocked and she opened the latch and stepped inside before she could second-guess herself.

Ada was in the kitchen, kneading dough for bread. At the sound of the door opening she spun around and raised the rolling pin that sat next to her hand. When she saw that it was Patience, her mouth dropped open and Patience swore there was a momentary gleam of happiness in her eye before her brain caught her up. "Get out!" Ada insisted.

Patience stood her ground. "I will not," she responded calmly. "Not until you listen to me."

"You have to go or the beast will eat you. He will!"

Shaking her head, Patience took a step into the kitchen, towards Ada. "I know," she said softly.

Ada's eyes widened. "Know what?" she murmured.

"I know that your beast is only a toy. It is like the cat I saw upstairs. I presume it has a key to wind it and it performs certain actions, but it is not a real beast." Patience stated, in a calm and measured voice.

"Oh...no...but..." Ada blanched and her knees started to shake visibly.

Patience hurried across the space that remained between them and got a chair under Ada just as she sank down. Patience turned and filled a glass of water from the sort-of pump she'd seen the first night, when Ada had filled the bath. She tested the water to make sure it was the cold and not the hot she was spilling into the glass and knelt beside Ada, lifting the glass to the girl's mouth. Ada's hand came up to hold the glass but she avoided touching Patience and Patience drew her hand back, confident that Ada had hold of it.

Ada sipped slowly, and a bit of color came back into her cheeks. Once she no longer looked in danger of toppling over, Patience stood and retreated a few steps to give Ada some room.

"Oh." The girl said again, once she had finished the water, as she turned around and looked for somewhere to put the glass. She was just a bit too far away to reach the worktable, so Patience took it from her and set it beside the forgotten dough.

Patience opened her mouth to say something reassuring but both girls' attentions were captured by the sound of tinkling glass coming from the front of the house. Patience hurried out into the hall, sensing Ada right behind her. They stopped short when they saw three large men coming through the front door, having unbolted it by reaching through the now broken window that was set into its upper part. Patience didn't know what to do. She stared at the men in confusion, then looked over her shoulder at Ada. She was fairly sure they shouldn't be here.

Ada was backing away, looking frightened. She didn't seem to know what to do either and Patience suddenly needed to do something.

"You had better turn around and walk back out

that door right now or the beast will eat you," she said. Even to herself her voice sounded shaky and uncertain and she tried to steady it. "He will tear you limb from limb."

The man in front leered at her. "Where is he then? I don't think he cares that we're here. Do you?" he asked his companions, who guffawed and walked toward the girls.

Ada disappeared back into the kitchen and Patience felt a moment of disappointment, thinking that the brunette had fled. Ada was back in a moment though, brandishing the rolling pin. "Get out of my house!" she demanded.

Good for her, Patience thought. But the girl's bravado didn't seem to make any difference. The three men continued walking slowly towards them. They backed away until they reached the wall. One of the men grabbed Patience's wrists and held them together, and although she struggled as hard as she could, he barely seemed to notice. The third man grabbed the rolling pin as it flew toward his head, and tore it from Ada's grasp. He grabbed her by both arms and she kicked him in the shin.

"Ye brat! I'll fix ye," he spat, striking Ada across the face. She didn't cry out but Patience could see her go pale again.

"Not now," the first man insisted, keeping his voice quiet. "If the beast hasn't heard us yet, he will if you beat the girl and she screams."

Patience felt rather like screaming herself but knew it would do no good. No one from outside would hear her and it would confirm to the men that the beast was not going to do anything. She bit her lip hard and continued struggling with her captor.

The lead man entered the kitchen and called out, "Bring them in here." Patience and Ada were drugged through the kitchen and tossed into the open door of the pantry. Patience fell, striking her knee hard as she heard the key turn on the outside. They were locked in.

"Ada, we need light." Patience thought there were probably candles stored somewhere in the room, but she had no idea where and no hope of finding them without light. Ada was still standing by the back shelves, but Patience couldn't see what she was doing. "Ada!" she insisted.

She could vaguely make out movement and a few moments later the sound of a match being struck was followed by a faint glow. Ada used the match's light to find a box of candles and lit one, then passed it to Patience, and lit a second for herself. Now comfortably bright, Patience looked around the room and confirmed that there was only the one door leading to the kitchen. She pushed at it, but the lock was strong and it didn't give. "Now what?" she asked.

Ada looked terrified. Her fighting spirit seemed to have fled once they were trapped. "I don't know. We have to get them out. I don't know what to do," she said, then stopped, listening.

Patience was silent while she waited for Ada to continue. Instead, the girl moved beside Patience, standing at the door and pressing her ear against it. Patience followed her lead and they could just hear the men's voices coming from the kitchen.

"I'm 'ungry." One of them complained. "Why don' we get 'em girls to make us somefink to eat?"

"Keep quiet," another said. "There's probably food in here, find yourself something but shh. We don't want the creature to know we're here."

The girls heard the sound of rummaging and a triumphant exclamation. They could only hear chewing for a while, and then one spoke again, clearly with his mouth full. "so wot's the plan agan?"

"Idiot," the leader hissed. "How many times do I have to tell you? We wait until night, until we're sure the creature's asleep. Then we find its den or room or whatever and kill it. Then we get this nice big house all to ourselves. Simple."

"But wot about 'em?"

"I'm sure we can find some use for those girls, don't you think?" he responded. "They were right pretty."

Patience stepped back from the door in horror. She didn't want to hear anything further. Ada stayed pressed against it, but there didn't seem to be any more conversation.

"What do we do?" Patience hissed, her stomach turning flip flops inside her.

Ada was silent, her hand pressed to her mouth, although whether to keep from screaming or throwing up Patience wasn't sure. In truth, she was half-tempted to do both of those things.

"We need to get them out. What can we do?" Patience repeated. "Can you actually make the creature kill someone?"

Shaking her head firmly, Ada finally looked at

her. "No. No, he can't do anything like that. You saw. he can only do those few things. Walk a bit, roar and turn his head around. That's all. I never thought to make him do more."

Patience swallowed past the lump in her throat. "We can't just stay here. I don't suppose you have a key to this door on you?"

"No, I never lock the inside doors of the rooms I use. The keys just stay in the locks usually. But I can get us out of here."

Patience looked around for another door she'd missed, but there wasn't one. "How?"

Ada walked to one of the shelves on the side walls, one that held sacks of apples and flour and other foodstuffs. She started removing the sacks carefully and placing them out of the way. Patience was still confused but started to help her. When the shelves were clear, Ada tugged at them, then tugged harder. The shelves moved a few inches away from the wall. She pulled again and Patience lent her whole strength as well. Between them they managed to swing the rack far enough from the wall that they could get behind. Ada squeezed in and opened a small door set about waist-high. Patience tried to determine where it went, but just saw a small space and darkness going up. "It's a dumbwaiter." Ada explained. "The dining room is on the first floor, and the kitchen staff sent the food into the room next to it so they wouldn't have to carry heavy serving trays up and down stairs. Father extended it up to the second floor, to the workshop. He got parts and liquids and things up that way."

Patience decided Ada's father was a very sensible man. "But, will it take us? We weigh rather more than serving platters do. And it looks terribly small."

Ada smiled a little, "I used to ride in it when I was a little younger. I pulled myself up and down to surprise my father. It would take my weight fine. And I know how to pull the ropes to get me up. I don't think we'd both fit, but if I go up first, I can send the platform down and pull you up after. At least we won't be trapped in here. Then we can sneak out of the house, maybe."

"We can't just run away, trust me. It's not at all fun. Especially if you aren't prepared for it. Do you know anyone nearby who will help you?" Patience queried.

Ada frowned. "No one knows I'm here, except one person. And I don't think he could do anything."

"Then we have to stay and do it ourselves," Patience resolved. "Let us get upstairs and see if we can find anything in that workshop to help us. There must be something." She helped Ada squeeze herself into the small opening. She was crouched on the platform with her knees nearly up to her ears, but she did fit. And her arms were free to pull up on the rope that was hanging in the corner. It took only a few moments until Ada pulled herself out of sight.

Patience walked back over to the door to see if she could hear anything else, but the men had either gone to sleep or were sitting in silence. She wished there was a way she could block the door to stop them seeing inside, so the men wouldn't know they had escaped. She tried to tug the shelf that they had moved to unblock the dumbwaiter and got it partway across the doorframe. She piled the sacks of food back on the shelves. It wouldn't entirely block the view from the kitchen, but it would make it harder for the men. They'd have to empty a shelf or two at least to see that the girls weren't hiding somewhere. Satisfied she returned to the little door just as the platform slid into place.

Praying to God to get them out of this safely, Patience folded herself up as compactly as she could in order to fit in the small space. She couldn't crouch like Ada, who was several inches shorter than she, but had to sit on the platform with her knees and neck touching and her skirts tucked in wherever there was room. It wasn't the least bit comfortable, and she was almost as relieved to exit into the workshop from the dumbwaiter as she was to be far from those nasty men.

She looked around and found Ada, who had stepped back to give Patience room to unfold herself. Her face showed the strain from the effort to pull both girls up two flights, but she had developed a resolved expression and waved her hands around the room in a welcoming gesture. "Let's see what we have to work with, shall we?"

CHAPTER ELEVEN

PATIENCE SPUN slowly in a circle trying to take in the myriad of tools, toys and liquids on the counters around her. Her eyes lit on the cat, drawn to its familiarity, and dismissed it as being unhelpful. No man was going to be frightened by a cat, real or otherwise. She shrugged and looked at Ada. "I don't know what most of this is, much less what we can do with it." Her ignorance galled her, but she hadn't had more than a few minutes in the room before Ada removed her, and Ada must know the contents intimately.

Ada looked like she was concentrating as she circled the room, looking at the objects and shaking her head as she decided against them. The first thing she stopped at was a stack of black metal boxes, the size of small loaves of bread. Ada fiddled with the top one for a moment and a very quiet lion's roar emerged from the side.

Patience asked "can that be made louder?"

Ada nodded and pushed a lever, restoring the box to a higher volume, "I put it on its quietest setting so they wouldn't hear it. But it's the same sort of thing that makes the beast roar. There's the lion, and also bats rustling, an owl hooting and some sort of eerie howling that I still haven't figured out. Father made recordings of all of the creatures and placed them in these boxes. They run on clockwork, like a music box, but sound very realistic and they're recorded at intervals, so there's a random time between sounds and there are variations. If we wind them up fully they will run for more than an hour before shutting down."

"That's fantastic. We can hide them in different rooms and the noises will seem to come out of nowhere. That will worry the men at least. Maybe scare them senseless. A lion roaring somewhere in the same house as me would certainly scare me. But I think we need something that will actually do some damage too, in case they are too stupid to get scared." Patience grinned and Ada responded with a lovely smile.

Ada patted the head of a stone dog, pulling it toward her. Then she set some sort of gear on the base behind it going and stepped back very quickly. The dog didn't do anything until Ada screwed up a ball of paper and tossed it in that direction. When it was about 6 inches away the dog suddenly flew into motion and snapped at it, biting the edge of the ball, which got stuck on a stone tooth. Reaching gingerly around the side, careful to let no part of her actually get in front of the statue, she halted the motion of the gear.

Ada said, "Father made this to keep nosy servants out of here, so they wouldn't know what he was working on. All it took was a single bite out of one young houseboy and none of the servants would come near this room again."

Patience stared at the dog, which once again looked completely motionless and was indistinguishable from regular stone. "How does it know where someone is?" she asked, keeping well away from the piece, even though Ada seemed to have turned it off.

Ada shrugged. "I haven't the foggiest idea. Father said something about sensing motion, but I never got around to asking him how it worked. Wish we had a dozen more of them though. This is the only one. It can't bite deeply enough to really injure someone, but it can certainly hurt and frighten them." She shook her head. "It should go somewhere they are definitely going to try to get into. It won't do anything unless someone is right in front of it." She took a few steps to her right. "Now, see this little bird in the cage?"

The cage was about two feet high and the bird no bigger than six or seven inches tall. Patience doubted it could do any harm to anyone, but she nodded at Ada.

"This creature makes the most appalling shriek when you attach a filament to the cage and it's broken. See, you put one end here, and stick the other end to a wall, low down so no one sees it."

She pulled a thin, translucent thread out of a small box sitting beside the cage and touched the end to Patience's hand to show how it was sticky. "It has to be taut, so when someone breaks the filament by stepping on it or into it, that sets the bird off. I've never heard anything so loud and annoying in my life. Father had this idea about keeping thieves out of houses, or scaring them off before they entered. I thought about using this before I came up with the beast to keep people away. I don't think it would have been as effective over a period of time as the beast though." She nodded in satisfaction. "At least, it worked until now," she muttered, looking at Patience, and then staring down at the floor as if she could see the men waiting down there.

Patience wandered over to the counter full of liquids and chemicals. "Can we do anything with these? Blow something up maybe?"

"Blowing things up is easy," Ada commented. "But then we'd have a blown-up house and still not be able to live in it. How would that help?"

Although disappointed that her idea wasn't useful, Patience focused on Ada's use of the word "we", and that thrilled her suddenly. Would Ada let her stay, if all this was successful? She hoped it wasn't just a slip of the tongue.

"Oh, but wait." Ada pulled a couple of jars close to her, and mixed their contents. Patience waited for something to happen, but the mixture just looked like a different color of liquid. Ada carried the jar over to a grey box, opened up a little funnel and poured the liquid in. "If we take this down and add some coals from the fire, it will spit out a foggy substance. It looks very creepy and otherworldly, and spreads out much more than steam would. And also, if it touches your skin it will sting. Badly enough that you need to wash it off with soap, just water won't clear it away. I think enough of it might cause a burn, but I've not tested it."

Patience tilted her head. "What did your father intend this one for?" she asked. She could see how it could be useful in their particular situation, but wasn't sure what other uses it could have.

Ada surprised Patience by blushing. "Well, actually, father built it as a sort of fog creating machine. For the stage, so there could be mist if the play was set in a graveyard or something. I was the one who created the liquid solution to make the stinging. I'm quite good with chemistry," she said.

In response, Patience touched Ada's hand. "It is brilliant," she said. "It is ever so much more useful this way."

Ada blushed deeper. "We'll see if all this works," she said, but she didn't move her hand away and looked at Patience with an unreadable expression. Patience met her gaze and, for a moment, forgot the urgency of their situation. She smiled and Ada smiled back in response, taking a small step towards her.

A thud came from below and they both stood up straight. "Is there anything else?" Patience asked.

Biting her lip, Ada turned around, her eyes darting over everything momentarily. Then her eyes lit up. "One more." She bent over and picked up a shiny metal cylinder that was attached to a cube about the width of a thick book. She placed the device on the counter and turned the cylinder several times. It made a clicking sound and when she let go it started to revolve very slowly. Patience tried to see what it was doing, but she couldn't figure it out. Ada went to the curtains, closed them tightly and pointed.

Across the wall an almost human shaped light moved slowly. It was fuzzy, but didn't flicker, it just seemed translucent. A shiver ran down Patience's spine, even though she knew the cylinder was the source of the light. It looked just as she had always expected a ghost to look, and behaved the same way. If she hadn't known better she would have been terrified. Ada let the cylinder run out and then opened the drape to let in a little more light.

"That should scare them some," she said, grinning widely.

Patience nodded. "It's very creepy. We should put it somewhere near the mist. Where are we going to place all these things?" she considered.

"Most of it had better go on the first floor. That's where they'll probably look for the beast."

"Where is it?" Patience asked, curious as to where it was kept when Ada wasn't trying to scare people off.

She shrugged. "It's in the room that you climbed into that first night. There's a cupboard in the corner that's inset into the wall and papered the same as the walls around it. It wouldn't conceal much if you had the window drapes open or electric lights on, but if it's dim it looks just like part of the wall. And it's locked." She pulled a key from under her dress and showed Patience. "I don't think they'll find it. They said they would go upstairs and kill him when he was asleep. Surely they'll wait until dark or even later. We need to have some idea when in order to wind up everything and get it started, otherwise things will run down before they can do their job."

Patience hadn't thought of that. "How will we find out?" she asked.

Ada shrugged. "Let's get things placed first and then worry about it. We'll think of something. We'll need a couple of minutes at least to run around and get stuff ready."

Nodding in agreement, Patience started lifting the sound boxes into her arms and then put them back on the counter. "Wait, take your shoes off so they do not hear us moving around. I will place the lion in the first room past the stairs up here; that should deter them from this floor. It would deter me. Hopefully that means they will concentrate on the first floor where the rest of the objects are."

Ada removed her shoes and went to pick up the fog machine but stopped before she touched it and dug in a small drawer under the counter until she emerged with a key. "This is a skeleton key. It'll fit any room in the house. In case you want to put anything into a room that's locked."

Patience juggled the boxes as she took the key and held it between her thumb and forefinger. She went out into the corridor, heard Ada following and gave her a quick smile over her shoulder before heading to the end of the hallway nearest the stairs.

As she unlocked the room there, Ada slid past her silently and padded down the stairs. Patience left the lion's box and locked the room behind her. The lion's roar wouldn't scare anyone if they could see that there was no lion to go with it.

She dropped off the other three boxes in likely-looking places, concealed but in places where the sounds would be audible. She didn't think the owl would scare anyone, but the odder the house seemed, the more likely to frighten the men off. She also turned the volumes up to near maximum. The louder, the better, she decided as she walked back up to the workshop. Deciding to leave the stone dog alone for now, she picked up the birdcage and met Ada on her way back into the room.

Ada was looking at the dog. "He should go somewhere they are definitely going to pass," she said.

"Put him right in the middle at the top of the stairs. Maybe he will make one of them fall and they will leave before anything else is needed." Patience suggested.

Ada looked a little shocked. "But if one falls on the stairs, he could get really hurt."

"They mean to hurt us. I would rather they were the ones to suffer than you or I. I do not think we can afford to be squeamish here."

"I'll take off the bulb at the top of the banister and put him there. It leaves it a little more to chance if one of them gets close enough to be bit, but it'll look more natural than if it sits on the floor in the middle of the stairs. And we don't want it to look as though we've set traps," Ada decided.

"That is true. Everything needs to look normal, so when the abnormal starts they will be more shocked." She hefted the birdcage and picked out a couple of the filaments from the box. She could only use one at a time but it never hurt to have extras. She listened carefully before descending the staircase to the first floor. Still nothing from below. With luck the men would wait until they were ready.

One of the parlours had a door that stood slightly open. Patience checked the fireplace to make sure that wasn't the room where Ada had hidden the fog machine. Finding it cold she placed the birdcage on a small table and dragged it close to the door. Then she attached the filament to the cage and pulled the other end right across the doorway. There was almost no way the men could miss tripping it if they went into the room. Stepping carefully she returned to the workshop and found Ada already there, looking at the ghost-cylinder and biting her lip.

"I don't know where to put this," she said. "It should be somewhere dim, but a place where they'll be for a few minutes so they have time to notice it."

Patience smiled wickedly. "Put it in the bedroom at the end. I will muss the sheets to make a nest and get it to look like someone was asleep there. Then, if they find the room they will think that is where the beast was, but will not know where it is now. Between that and the ghost, it should finish them off. I hope."

Ada nodded. "It could work. We still have to know when they're coming up so we can get everything started and hide. The dog is ready, but everything else needs preparation."

"I was thinking about that," Patience mused. "If you lower me back down to the pantry, I can listen for them and when they start talking about leaving I can yank the rope, so you know to pull me back up."

Ada considered. "It would make more sense for me to be down there. Tugging on the rope would be a good signal, but you could start setting things while I pull myself back up. Unless you think you could get as far as the first floor yourself."

Patience frowned. "I doubt I am strong enough," she admitted. "I never had to do much lifting or pulling. I could wait down there and let myself out into the kitchen after they left." She didn't like the idea of Ada being down where the men were. She didn't much like the idea for herself either, but it seemed the better option. After all, Ada was the one who knew better how everything worked.

Ada discarded the idea with a shake of her head. "I won't have time to get everything started by myself. If we assume they'll take a couple of minutes to look through the ground floor rooms we can do it together, but with just me it'd be too risky. I'll go down. I'll only have to get to the first floor, not all the way back up here. It'll only take a minute or two. You take the cylinder and get everything set up. Then go to the serving area next to the dining room and hold the rope. I'll tug 3 times when I want you to get started. Don't worry about the fog machine, I'll do that one. The rest you already know how to wind up. Make sure you turn the keys as many times as they'll let you. We want the longest use out of everything."

Patience picked up the cylinder. "I hope we will not scare ourselves with all the noise," she commented.

Ada held up a handful of something that looked like bread dough. She pulled off two wedges and handed them to Patience. "Put these in your ears. They'll block out some of the noise. That bird'll give you a headache for a week, even from upstairs."

Patience rolled the stuff between her fingers and mimicked Ada, placing it in both ears. "Good?" she asked, and was surprised that she could barely hear her voice.

Ada nodded. "Good luck," she mouthed.

"You too."

Patience spontaneously gave Ada a hug. For a moment the girl stiffened and then her arms went around Patience in return. Patience gave her a quick peck on her cheek and almost ran out the door, not wanting to see Ada's reaction.

She slowed as she neared the staircase, and climbed down very carefully, knowing she wouldn't be able to hear if the men were on their way up until they surprised her. The sun was just setting, and she hoped they'd stay in the kitchen for long enough. She hurried down the corridor and prepared the furthest room in the way she'd said. She pulled all the covers off the bed, and dropped them in one corner. Then she lay down in the pile and wiggled around to leave the impression of a large body. She pulled one wardrobe door slightly open and then looked around for a good place to leave the cylinder. It would be best if it was somewhere in the center of the room, but there wasn't any furniture there that she could use to prop it up.

Finally, she put it on the dressing table and decided that was better than nothing. She dropped a lampshade half over it, not enough to disrupt the light, but enough to give it some camouflage. Then she found the dining room and the serving area next to it, opened the door to the dumbwaiter and held the rope lightly, waiting for Ada's signal. With her ears stopped up she could hear the blood pounding through her veins as her heart rate sped up in fear. There was the thumping from her heart and an almost rushing sound, and beyond that she couldn't hear anything. She found that almost as disconcerting as the length of the wait.

The rope jerked in her hand. She waited for the second and third yank to ensure that it was time and then ran. She started with the ghost machine and then went around turning on the various sounds, intending to end with the lion. She saw Ada go into one room, and she knew that the fog machine would be ready. Her heart still beat strongly as she ran up the stairs to the second floor and her hands were shaking badly enough that it took her a moment to get the key in the lock.

By the time she'd wound the lion up, Ada had passed the open door and was in the workshop. She locked the room behind her and followed the other girl. She could hear the lion, even through the stuff in her ears. It was much louder than the other sound boxes. Even expecting it, and with her hearing diminished, she still jumped the first time the sound played. Ada noticed and grinned. Patience watched her until she saw Ada jump too.

Something occurred to her. She looked around and located a piece of paper and a pencil. "How will we know if it works?" she wrote.

Ada took the pencil from her hand. "I didn't think of that. Maybe we could hide near the top of the stairs. We won't know what's going on from here."

Patience didn't like not knowing. They could sit in that room for ages, and then get surprised by the men. She opened the door and fished the putty from one ear. Faintly she could hear the owl, but only the lion was very loud from her position and she could not determine where the men might be.

Suddenly there was a sharp yelp from down the stairs. A man's voice, loud enough to hear spoke. "Tha' statue's alive!" He sounded scared. If there was a reply, it was too low to hear but it didn't sound like they'd abandoned the house. Not yet.

Patience grinned widely at Ada, who raised her eyebrow. Patience mimed a bite with her teeth and Ada nodded in understanding. She pulled out the putty from one ear as well and they listened further. When nothing except their machines made any noise, Patience tiptoed to the end of the hallway, and crouched down, peering between the posts of the banisters and trying to make out what was happening. She could see the very top of the stone dog's head, but the men weren't there anymore. She figured they were going into the rooms on the floor where she couldn't see them.

A piercing wail came screaming up at them. One of them must have found the bird. Quickly Patience stuck the putty back in her ear. It would prevent her from knowing what was happening downstairs, but Ada hadn't exaggerated the volume of that creature. Even through the plugs, the wailing was loud enough to wake the dead. She couldn't imagine what the men might be hearing. She strained her eyes, trying to see around a corner. The lion roared again, more sustained this time and one man ran down the stairs toward the front door. He was screaming something but she couldn't hear what it was. She suspected they might be words she wasn't supposed to know anyway.

She waited for the other two men to follow but they did not.

She squinted a little and thought she could make out some mist, just coming into view. She wondered if that was what had driven the first man out. A shriek came from below. She braved the bird sound and pulled the putty out again.

"It burns!" the man said, sounding almost panicked. It sounded like the same man who'd gotten bit by the dog. He couldn't be having a good day.

Patience smiled evilly.

Another man's voice joined his. "It only stings a bit, it won't hurt you. Try to stay out of the smoke." He was the one with the better class of voice, the one who seemed to be the leader. "Go and try the rest of the doors on that side. I'll try these."

"But Jake 'ready tried 'em. The're locked," the insistent voice whined. "It ent worth it. I wanna go."

"You'll stay here and do your job or you'll regret

it. I promise you that," the leader sounded angry.

"Jake ent here either."

"And Jake will regret that. Go do what I say."

Patience looked to see if the man would defy the order, but no one else went down the stairs. She heard a thump and then another one. The man seemed to be trying to knock a locked door down. Patience knew that the doors in this house were solid and all he'd do was bruise his shoulder unless he was very strong. None of the men had seemed particularly big, and she doubted it would work.

She very much wanted to put the putty hack in her ear, the bird sound pained her, but not knowing what was happening was too frightening. Ada still had both ears blocked and was wincing every so often, but was watching Patience more than she was looking downstairs.

Patience shrugged. She didn't know what was happening.

There came a triumphant shout, though it faded away quickly. One of the men must have found the room they'd set up as the beast's. She rose quickly, and hurried down the hallway to the workshop, pulling Ada after her. She closed the workshop door and went to the fireplace, listening carefully. She'd noticed earlier that they shared a chimney and thought she might be able to hear what was happening. She pulled the putty from her other ear and crouched down, her head almost in the grate.

She felt something brush her hair aside, and then Ada was holding it in her hand, trying to keep it out of the ashes. She took the plait from Ada and held it herself, ignoring the tingling that she'd felt when Ada had brushed her ear as she gathered it. She couldn't stop a small smile though, as she tried to focus.

Sounds did carry, though not very well. "...was here." She heard and then, "Where...now?" The first voice, the leader sounded a little worried. The second voice sounded almost panicky. "...find it...upsters..." came up.

She frowned and waited to see if there was anything else.

"Ahhhhh." The scream was even louder than the bird, for a moment. Patience heard boots pounding down the hallway, and presumably down the stairs, though she couldn't quite make that out. She opened the workshop door. Just then, the lion roared again. It blended with the bird in a weird sort of harmony. That seemed to do it. A second set of boot thumps followed the first, punctuated by a yelp in the middle.

The leader must have run into the dog again on his way out. She ran to the stairs and saw him just as he jumped down the final few steps and flew towards the front.

Ada hadn't followed her and when Patience went looking for her she found Ada looking out a front window. "They've all gone. It worked!" She was almost bouncing and tears were streaming down her face.

Patience didn't know what to do. She wanted to dance in a circle and shout for joy and shut that bird up, but she didn't know which to do first. Without thinking, she put her arms around Ada to hug her and found her mouth on the dark-haired girl's. Her brain stopped working for a moment. Then, once it registered what she was doing, she waited to be slapped.

Part of her wanted to turn and run, embarrassed and scared and unsure, but by the time she'd sorted out the emotions it was too late. Ada had stiffened as Patience touched her, but to Patience's shock she neither moved away nor struck.

Patience felt a tentative touch on her cheek. Ada's hand was touching her, and she definitely wasn't trying to push her away. Patience gave in to her body's desire and both hands held Ada tighter, one on the back of her head, and the other on her waist. She let her eyes drift shut and for a little while, all she could feel was the girl's lips. Softer than anything she'd ever felt. Her waist was small and warm and Patience never wanted to let go.

She wished to stay there for a hundred years and spend the rest of her life in the kiss. It would be a wonderful life.

Slowly, she felt Ada start to step back. She held on more tightly for a moment but then let go. Was she going to get hit now? She opened her eyes to see Ada looking at her. Surprise warred with gentleness on the beautiful face and Patience waited, more terrified now than she had been of the men.

Ada didn't put her out of her misery quickly. She was silent for what felt like an hour, but she didn't step any further from Patience, nor did her face display unhappiness. Patience's heart felt like it might burst from the waiting.

"We should turn off the machines." Ada

suggested softly, her eyes never leaving Patience's. The lion's roar punctuated her statement.

Patience nodded.

Ada turned from Patience and went to the door. "Keep out of the mist," she reminded Patience, as she slipped through.

Patience's eyes followed her. Her fingers rose to touch her bottom lip, which felt warm and tingly. The rest of her felt cold though, without Ada there to keep her warm. She didn't know what Ada meant to do now. Maybe she was just putting off the inevitable.

Patience's steps were leaden as she went into the corridor. Ada was already downstairs, so she went to the lion's room and unlocked it, turning off the noise box and carrying it carefully back to the workshop. She was procrastinating going downstairs but she had a job to do so she steeled her shoulders and descended.

The other boxes were quickly gathered, and Patience had all of them stacked up when Ada emerged from the room at the end of the hall, carrying the ghost machine. Their eyes met and Ada smiled softly. Patience felt like she could breathe again, a weight removed from her chest. She almost ran back up the stairs with the boxes, as Ada followed her more slowly, carrying the ghost cylinder and the birdcage, which mercifully, she'd shut off first.

"We need to let the steam run out and dissipate some before I can bring the fog machine back." Ada spoke, as she placed the birdcage back in its spot on the counter.

Patience nodded.

"It will take a while, maybe an hour. Until then we should try not to go near the room. Maybe we could go down to the kitchen and make something to eat?" she suggested.

Patience nodded again, still waiting for Ada to say something about the kiss. Her heart still thudded and she wanted to touch the girl again. She didn't trust herself to speak until she knew it would be okay. Her eyes avoided Ada's, as she carefully stacked the noise boxes, lining them up perfectly and then looking around for anything else that would keep her busy.

Ada walked over and stood beside her for a moment, then took Patience's hand. "Come on," she tugged the blonde behind her.

CHAPTER TWELVE

ADA HELD her hand all the way down to the kitchen and only let go when she had to light the stove. Patience dropped her hand to her side, feeling very unsettled and anxious. She looked around for something to do and noticed how messy the kitchen was. If there had been bread in the breadbox, it was gone, only minuscule crumbs remained. The empty rind on the counter suggested the cheese had met a similar fate. The men had clearly eaten everything they could find and had made a terrible mess besides. She picked up a cloth and swept the crumbs from the table into her hand, then looked around, unsure of where to deposit them.

Ada saw her looking and gestured to the door, "Just toss them outside. The birds will enjoy them," she said, sounding quite pleased. Patience did as she was told and then found a broom in a tiny cupboard and swept the floor, sweeping those crumbs out the door as well.

Ada had unlocked the pantry and giggled. "What did you do?" she asked.

Patience remembered that she had moved the shelf to block the door after Ada went up in the dumbwaiter, but was a little surprised that she hadn't noticed when she returned to the pantry. Then she realized Ada hadn't had a candle and had probably never gotten out of the dumbwaiter. "I thought they might come and check on us so I tried to make it harder for them," she admitted.

Ada tried pushing the shelf back to where it belonged but couldn't get a purchase on it. "You did. But now you'll have to come help me put it back or we won't have any dinner."

Patience stood beside her, carefully keeping her elbows in so she didn't touch Ada by accident. Ada showed no such compunction and together they managed to slide the shelf back to the wall where the dumbwaiter hid, and replaced the sacks on the shelves. Ada filled a small basket with fruit and vegetables, another bread loaf and a cheese, carrying it into the kitchen, Patience following behind.

"It's really too late to start a big meal, don't you think? Will this be enough for you?" Ada asked, retrieving a knife from the knife block and laying out the vegetables onto the table to chop.

Patience's stomach was still feeling butterflies and she wasn't sure she could eat anything until Ada said something about the kiss, but she nodded, and set herself to cutting up chunks of apple and pear while

Ada focused on the vegetables. They took two plates from a sideboard and helped themselves to some food.

Patience decided she needed to think of something else and she realized she knew almost nothing about Ada, except that her father was an inventor who was missing, and that she was good at chemistry. All the times they'd talked before, Ada had been more than happy to discuss books and flowers and everything else, but had really said very little about herself.

"Can you tell me why you made the beast-creature?" Patience asked, toying with a slice of apple.

Ada seemed uncomfortable, and Patience wished she hadn't said anything.

"It was so I could stay here." Ada said, not looking at Patience.

She seemed to be waiting, and Patience asked, "What do you mean?"

Ada took a deep breath and started her story. "I was born in this house. My father is an inventor, which you know. And my mother came from a wealthy family in London. I don't even know how they met. It must have been in London, there was no reason for her to be here. No one really comes to the village. Anyway, they fell in love and she came to live in the house when they were married. The house belonged to my father's parents, so I guess they had some money too, but I don't know where from. They died long before I was born. My mother's mother died when I was a baby, and I think her father shortly after. I can't remember them at all, though my father says I met them.

My mother died when I was just a girl, I think I told you that once," she looked up at Patience, the faintest glimmer of tears in her eyes. "I know I loved my mother, she was so beautiful, but I worshiped my father. I wanted to be just like him, and I think I took after him too. I learned to read very young and he was forever bringing books home for me and for himself. Well, you've seen his library.

My mother made sure I didn't neglect myself, I think because she couldn't really do anything about him. He forgets to eat unless someone puts food right in front of him, and sometimes even then. Our cook was very good, but sometimes he was thinking so hard about a problem he would hold a forkful of food in front of his mouth for minutes at a time but he'd forget to open his mouth and put in. It was quite funny," she giggled a little.

"Anyway, my mother ensured I was dressed properly and made sure I ate regularly and it all went quite well, even if I did take after my father. Twice a year we took a trip into London to stay with her older sister, who never married. She lived in the house that had been their parents', and was very proper and ladylike. My mother was too, of course, but not as cross about it. My aunt Euphania, she didn't care for me at all. My father encouraged me to talk, you see. And I had opinions about everything, which he thought was grand. My aunt did not. She thought little girls should be seen and not heard, which was how she'd been brought up. My father and she fought horribly, until he refused to go to London at all with Mother and me. And my mother was caught in the middle. She was a little frightened, I think, of Euphania and would always promise to take me to nice places if I did what I was expected to do."

Patience understood exactly what Ada meant about family expecting her to be the sort of girl she wasn't naturally inclined to be. She nodded and Ada nodded back, commiserating with Patience's own childhood.

"Anyway, my mother died, as I said, and although I was very sad, I managed to get through it. Aunt Euphania wanted me to come live with her, she didn't think my father would bring me up as befitted my station, but he put his foot down and refused to speak about it. After the funeral, I only saw my Aunt once a year, when he sent me to London to stay with her. The last time I saw her was just after I refused to go back again, she arrived here expecting to take me away permanently.

"They argued loudly enough for the whole village to hear and he sent her away, saying that I could choose when I was older if I wanted to live with her. Of course I didn't, and I refused to go see her again. I was afraid that she'd keep me in London and I'd never get to come home again. And I hated the way I had to be there. Wearing proper clothes and sitting quietly and the other girls she'd invite over for visiting and tea were so prissy and stuck up and didn't think of anything at all. They only cared about having their hair done just right and a new wardrobe made up each season. I never had a single thing to say to any of them."

Ada might as well be speaking about Patience's life. She understood exactly how the girl had felt. Except she hadn't had a loving parent and a safe home to go back to. She hadn't had any choice. "Did you want to go to school?" she asked.

"I expected to. Father arranged tutors for me. Not governesses, but real tutors like your brother had. And we studied all the things I would need to go to a university. Maybe Oxford, I thought. I didn't want to go to London because then I'd have to live with my Aunt."

Ada smiled, remembering. "I thought I was so clever, I'd play tricks on the tutors or hide in a tree if I didn't feel like studying what they wanted me to. But I usually worked hard to make my father proud of me. And in exchange he let me act however I wanted. Not to be rude or disobedient, but I didn't have to dress like a lady. I sometimes wore boys' clothes when I was younger, but I thought it'd be better if I started dressing like a girl when I was twelve or thirteen. That way no one in the village said anything nasty to me. They used to, sometimes, when I was a child. But mostly I didn't care." She clenched her teeth and Patience thought that she must have cared some, or she wouldn't have mentioned it.

"Anyway. I didn't have a lot of friends in the village. The girls were boring Band the boys wouldn't let me play with them, so usually I stayed home and talked to my father and my tutors.

My father has this friend, Mr. Welsh. He's the village blacksmith, but really he's a clock maker. He went to the University of London and had a shop in

London for a few years, but came back here when his father died, so he could take over the workshop and care for his mother. Mr. Welsh usually visits Father a few evenings a week and they have debates about everything. What they read in the paper or astronomy or politics or even suffragettes. My father calls me his little suffragette, sometimes," she smiled wistfully.

"They let you listen while they talked?" Patience inquired. It sounded so, since Ada knew what they talked about.

The girl grinned. "Let me listen? They encourage me to debate along with them. My father made sure I read the paper every week since I was six years old and quizzes me about the contents. He thinks girls should know as much as boys, which is more than most. He taught me to look at an issue from all sides and assigns me a debating side, even sometimes one that I don't believe in. My tutors also thought girls should be well-informed. I guess Father wouldn't have hired them otherwise.

"So I debate Father and Mr. Welsh, and sometimes make them see my viewpoint on issues. It was so different from how my mother was raised, she said. But she let my father teach me, even though sometimes she didn't understand what I was talking about. She did read, but mostly histories and nothing about technology or science. She said those things didn't interest her, but that it was okay if they interested me. Only she made me promise not to say anything to my Aunt about votes for women or going to university. She didn't want the fight."

Patience was envious. "I wish my father talked to me. I mostly only remember him chastising me for not sitting still enough in church or getting my dress dirty, when he noticed. Mostly he just patted me on the head and sent me away when I would ask him anything. And I was not supposed to read the paper, though sometimes Mason brought it to me. My father and your aunt probably would get along beautifully."

"I suppose they would, though she'd not speak to him much. She doesn't feel it's proper for an unmarried woman to speak to a man, except in passing. And only if they were properly introduced. She'd probably like your mother though, if she is as interested in dresses and marriages as you said."

"But she's left you alone since that last visit. Hasn't she?" Patience asked.

Ada nodded. "Because of my father. But if she knew my father... wasn't here right now, she'd insist on my coming to live with her. And I just couldn't. That's why."

Patience had gotten a little bit lost. "That's why what?" she asked.

"That's why I made the beast," Ada replied, quietly. "So I didn't have to go away." She wiped a tear from her eye, and Patience wanted to comfort her, but she needed to hear the rest of the story and maybe Ada needed to tell it.

"Father goes away quite regularly. Usually only for a few days, but it isn't terribly uncommon for him to be gone two weeks or a month. When my mother was alive she would look after me, and after she died, there were always servants who lived in the house and kept me safe. I was lonely while he was away but he'd always bring me something when he returned. A clockwork toy or new books, he knows what I like best. And he needs to travel to get supplies for his inventions, or to try and sell them. I know he took out patents on dozens of things and some of them have been manufactured. He's very smart."

"Of course he is," Patience assured her. "I've seen some of this things."

"Oh yes, that's right," Ada smiled. "They came in handy. Anyway, he shows me how he makes them, and I help him, especially with little tiny gears and cogs and things. My hands are quite steady." She held them up to show Patience, though they were shaking a little now. "He was here for my nineteenth birthday, he bought me a whole new set of clock tools, but when he left the last time, he said he'd be gone about a month. Maybe as much as two. I know he was going to the continent, Germany and a few other places. And I waited for him to come back, but he was gone so long that the servants started to talk. They said he probably wasn't going to come back. The nicer ones whispered that he must have been waylaid and murdered. Some of the others said he'd just run off. Of course, none of them said anything to me, but I could hear them whispering. And they'd always stop talking when I entered a room. None of them had been here that long, the cook we had since I was a child had retired to the country just before he left, and the others were always coming in and out. But when he'd been gone four or five months they started drifting away and I got worried. What would I do if they all left? I had some money, so I kept paying their wages, but no one wanted to work for a girl with no parents here to oversee the household. And when there were only a few left, and I knew they'd soon go, I had to think of something to keep my aunt from hearing anything and coming for me.

"The village has an old wives tale about a beast that lives in the woods." She waved towards the back door. "A horrible beast who eats anyone that crossed its path. They say he used to come to the village and steal goats or a calf, even a child or two. I don't know when the story started, long before I was born. Most people don't go too far into the woods. If they go in at all its just to cut a tree or two, and never alone."

"That's why I never saw anyone," Patience mused.

"Right, even now people are silly enough to believe things like that, when if they read a book once in a while they'd know that all the creatures in England have been identified and there are no such things as beasts in the woods. Wolves, sure, or other animals, but not any kind of supernatural thing." Ada frowned dismissively. "So you and I know there are no beasts, but no one else seemed to, so I decided that if they thought the beast had come here and eaten me, then they'd stay away."

Patience forbore to mention that she had believed in the beast too, when she'd heard the roaring and seen the creature Ada had made. She didn't want the girl to think less of her. And if Ada was willing to forget that she'd been as gullible as the villagers, she didn't want to remind her.

"I watched my father make the toy cat, you were right when you said it was just the same." Ada smiled a bit. "It was just much, much bigger. We had all the pieces around. Even the fur, though I only had just enough of that and had to glue most of it to the front. If someone saw it well from the back they'd realize it was awfully threadbare. I used a tiger's roar, but I slowed the mechanism a little to make it deeper and more sonorous. And I disappeared. I stopped going to the village for supplies just a few days before I brought the beast out for the first time. Luckily we have that good garden in the back, so I can get a lot of food from there. And I already knew how to trap animals. My father took me to the woods as a child, I wasn't scared! And he showed me about snares and knots and how to skin a rabbit. The cook taught me to pluck a chicken. She thought even the mistress of a house should know how to do everything. It's a very good thing she thought that or I'd have been useless alone." Ada bit her lip, and looked unhappy.

Patience tried to distract her. "But there must be things you need to buy. I know there are things you can't grow here." She was shaky on what exactly could be grown, but she knew flour and oats required much more space than a small garden could provide.

"That's where Mr. Welsh comes in. He's the only one who knows I'm here. He doesn't like it at all, but I told him that if he didn't help me I'd run away and live on the streets in a city and who knows what would happen to me. He wouldn't let me go. If he had a wife he might have sent her to look after me, but she passed away about the same time as my mother so it's just him and his son. And so he takes deliveries for me, and brings things I can't grow here, and occasionally a treat. He doesn't come often, though, he won't even tell his son; we never got on. But he tries to look after me, and makes sure I'm okay. And I was okay, I really was," she insisted.

Patience covered Ada's hand on the table. "Of course you are okay. It is quite amazing how you have managed. I would never be able to do what you did. And I understand why you did not want me to know about the beast, you barely know me and could not know that I would never speak your secrets to someone. But I promise I never will."

Ada clutched Patience's hand hard enough to hurt. "But they came. The men came and they'll tell everyone and ruin everything. What are we going to do?"

Ada had been so strong, since the moment Patience met her. She'd looked after herself and she'd looked after Patience and she'd come up with all the ideas of how to scare the intruders away, so Patience was astonished when the girl burst into uncontrollable tears. She went from storytelling to full out sobbing in moments. Patience didn't know what to do. She held Ada's hand and try to reassure her.

"The men are gone. Long gone," she told Ada. "They were so scared that they will never come back here. I suspect that they have not stopped running yet. You did not know them, so they cannot be from the village. No one there will ever know. And if they did find out, all you have done is made the story stronger. Not only is there a ferocious beast living here, but a lion and bats and ghosts. No one will ever come here again, certainly." There was no way to really be sure, but Ada certainly didn't need to hear that. "They are far away and will not return." She sounded as firm as she could.

"They'll take me away. They'll take me away to my Aunt and I'll never be here again. I won't be here when my fa...father comes back and he won't know where I am. I have to stay here until he comes back," Ada insisted.

"No one knows that you are here. You are safe. We will be safe," she repeated.

Ada only sobbed louder. "I don't want to go away."

Patience didn't even think Ada remembered she was there, but she put her arms around the sobbing girl and rocked her and patted her back and tried to make her stop crying. Nothing seemed to work. Ada was shivering the way Patience had when she'd first come, but she couldn't have caught a chill in the house. The sobbing went on and on and on and the shivering got worse.

Finally, Patience decided she had to do something. She stood and half picked Ada up until the girl was standing. She put both arms around Ada and led her from the kitchen thinking she needed to be somewhere warm, where she felt safe. She was outside in the corridor before she realized she didn't know where Ada slept. She couldn't leave her alone to go searching so she guided Ada up the stairs to the room she had been sleeping in. She sat Ada on the bed and pulled off her boots, tucking them neatly away. Then she pulled the covers back and lay Ada down, covering her with the heavy duvet. She smoothed Ada's hair away from her brow, and stroked her face, trying to be calming.

When she removed her hand to go fetch a chair to sit in, Ada cried harder so she sat on the edge of the bed and kept stroking her hair, a gesture she remembered some of the nurses and servants doing for her when she'd wept after being punished by her father.

Eventually, Ada's sobs slowed. Her eyelids became heavy, then closed and she seemed to fall asleep. Patience stayed where she was for a while, and then realized she too was chilled. She built a fire in the grate, and, looking back to make sure Ada was still asleep, she returned to the kitchen to boil some water for tea. While she waited she tidied up the kitchen and found the teapot and the chest where the leaves were. Luckily, it was unlocked. In her own house her mother kept a key to that and the salt chest. Just in case some servant might want more than their share.

While the water was heating, Patience went to look at the front door. The door itself was unbroken, though the pane of glass beside it had been shattered to allow the men to unbolt the lock. She thought for a minute and then wrestled a long table in the corridor up on its side covering most of the door and the glass panes to cover the hole. It wasn't a good solution but it would have to do for now. They could find wood and nails and board it up properly the next day. When she returned to the kitchen she poured the boiling water into the pot and put everything on a tray to take upstairs. She wanted to be there in case Ada woke up, she didn't know what else to do. She thought about the soup Ada had made her on the first night, but it didn't seem like it would help, even if she knew how. Tea would have to do, for now.

She couldn't have been gone more than ten minutes and Ada was still sleeping, her face flushed and wet with tears. She sat at the table where they had breakfast together and drank her tea. She had nothing to do but watch Ada sleep. She let herself stare longer than she would otherwise. Even red and damp, Ada still managed to be beautiful. Her eyes darted around under her eyelids, and her expression still looked anxious, but there was something that drew Patience to her, visible even in distress.

She wanted to protect Ada but she didn't know how. The girl had done everything to protect herself, and she probably would have gone on for a long time if those men hadn't come. Patience had never been so angry with anyone before. Not even with her father for insisting she marry a man she detested. If they had ruined everything, she would hunt them down and hurt them. She didn't know how, but she'd do it if Ada needed her to. Her fists clenched in her lap.

Patience was staring out the window at the moon when Ada cried out. Patience strode to the bed and put her hand on Ada's. "Shh, you are fine," she promised in a calm voice.

Both of Ada's hands clutched her own and she moaned. "They'll take me away," she whispered, tears starting to leak out of her eyes again. Patience didn't know why Ada was so fixated on this idea but she allowed Ada to clutch at one hand while her other resumed stroking Ada's hair.

"I will not let them," she promised. "I will never let them take you away."

Ada quieted down but the tears still streamed from her eyes and her shivering was so strong the whole bed shook. Patience looked around for something else to cover Ada to warm her but she could see nothing. The fire was still going strong and the room didn't feel chill to Patience, but Ada seemed to think otherwise. Patience wrapped her arms around Ada's shoulders and tried to keep her still but it didn't seem to help.

Finally, she kicked off her boots, gently pushed Ada over and climbed under the covers next to her. She leaned against the wall and held the girl, guiding her head to rest on Patience's shoulder. Ada put both arms around Patience and clutched her fervently; hard enough that Patience could feel individual fingers through her dress and shift. Eventually she slid down the wall until she was lying beside Ada, and rubbing her back with the arm that wasn't under her. She thought Ada had fallen asleep again when her hold loosened, and looked at her in the light of the fire.

Ada's eyes were open, and though they still

shone, there were no more tears.

"It will all be fine," Patience reassured her. "I am here with you." She wasn't sure if Ada was listening, but she seemed calmer anyway, and the shivering had stopped. Their eyes met and they both held still. Patience held her breath, waiting to see what Ada would do next.

Ada studied Patience's face. "You'll be here?" she asked.

Patience nodded, not trusting her voice. She realized exactly how close they were, and loosened her hold slightly, in preparation to move a little away. Ada's arm tightened on her to keep her in place, as though she knew what Patience was thinking. Her eyes returned to Patience's, unblinking, and then she pushed herself up on one elbow and kissed Patience's lips.

Patience couldn't help the sigh that escaped her. Ada seemed to take it as encouraging. She pressed her lips more firmly and put her free hand on Patience's cheek, where it had rested the first time Patience had kissed her. Patience had been lightly stroking Ada's back, before she was surprised into stillness. Now, her hand pressed more firmly as it moved up and down Ada's spine. She wanted to touch Ada's face, but her other hand was trapped under the girl and she didn't want to break the kiss by trying to free it. She rested her hand on Ada's hip and squeezed lightly, circling her fingertips over the thin cotton of the dress.

Ada moaned slightly into Patience's mouth, sending shivers down her spine. She focused on the feeling of Ada's lips against hers, moving gently. Tentatively, she touched the tip of her tongue to Ada's lip, feeling something reverberate through her when Ada opened her mouth in response. She realized she actually had no idea what she was doing. Her body was leading, but she didn't know where. It was beyond her strength to try and break away. She lightly stroked her tongue inside Ada's mouth, unsure how the girl would respond.

Ada pressed harder into her, her elbow giving way so her body was lying almost on top of Patience's chest. The weight didn't crush her, it sent another shiver through her, and her hand on Ada's hip shifted to the dip in her back just above her buttocks, pulling more tightly, until it felt like they were merged. She dug her hand out from between them and stroked Ada's face, her hair, her neck and her shoulders. Ada's right hand came up to cradle Patience's face and as she explored, Ada's hips pressed into Patience's, until there she found a leg in between her own.

Patience caught Ada's lip between her teeth and sucked on it, feeling pressure building deep inside her. Ada's back arched and Patience examined the expression on her face. Ada looked like nothing she had seen before. It was something akin to ecstasy, but earthier, more human than anything she recognized. Her whole body burned, the weight of her clothes and the bed covers dug into her. Ada's weight felt like a feather.

Fearlessly, Patience's hand dipped lower, pressing on the skin of Ada's chest above her dress, and then drifted to her breast, feeling the smooth cloth that separated then, and beneath it the hard outline of Ada's nipple. Ada gasped, grinding her breast into Patience's hand. Taking this for approval, Patience let her hand slide beneath the fabric, wanting nothing more than to feel the feverish skin below her fingers. The neckline was too high to expose much to her seeking fingers, but the skin of her breast was softer than she could have imagined.

She sucked at Ada's lip again, then thrust her tongue into the warm mouth, desiring to taste everything. Her hand strained and she pulled it from the dress's neck. Ada moaned in disappointment, but sucked her breath in as Patience's fingers untied the top of her gown. She pulled the laces from hole after hole until the dress was undone to Ada's waist. She wore only a loose shift closed with a single tie beneath, and Patience pushed the top of the dress and shift together over Ada's narrow shoulders. She could feel the girl trembling, but Ada raised herself from Patience's chest to allow her dress to be pushed to her waist, baring her breasts and stomach to Patience's view. She left off once the dress had reached Ada's hips, not wanting to rush anything, but her eyes took in the smooth skin that was only inches from her and Patience rose up to meet the pale expanse.

She kissed Ada over her heart, and one hand returned to Ada's back, keeping their hips pressed firmly together, while touching Ada's shoulder lightly with the other. That hand moved gently, wanting to caress every inch of skin above her. Ada arched her back again and this put her nipple within reach of Patience's mouth. Without stopping to question herself, her tongue darted out to taste the flesh, and swooped over the small button. Ada almost shrieked at the contact and dropped herself closer to Patience's seeking mouth.

Patience sucked the nipple into her mouth and then laved around it with her tongue. The flesh hardened further and the aureole contracted until Patience could feel individual bumps. At the same time her hand covered the other breast and her fingertip circled the nipple, stopping to weigh the orb and then teasing with her nail.

Although she'd never before touched anyone else this way, Patience's own nipples were very sensitive, and from the reaction she assumed Ada felt the same. After a few minutes she shifted her mouth to lick between her breasts and then raised her head to kiss Ada again deeply.

Ada's hands seemed to be everywhere, stroking Patience's sides and occasionally brushing over her breasts. Patience wanted more. She wanted nothing between them and her dress seemed very inconvenient at that moment. She slowly shifted, easing Ada to a sitting position without breaking the kiss and fumbled at the laces of her own dress, which did up the front.

Ada realized what she was doing and her fingers joined Patience's, fumbling with laces and mostly tying them in knots. There was no way for both girls to work at them at the same time without their fingers getting more tangled than the laces. Ada let

Patience deal with them while she ran her fingers through the larger girl's hair. Patience almost swooned, but eventually managed to detangle the mess that her laces were in and pulled them out of each eyelet deliberately. She couldn't get the bottom ones out, as Ada was now sitting on her lap, but undid what she could. Ada pushed the dress off Patience's shoulders and then tugged the chemise up from the waist, pulling it over Patience's head. Patience rolled from one hip to the other, and managed to get the rest of her dress off, taking her pantaloons and petticoats with it. Ada used the moment she was separated from Patience to push her dress and shift down to her ankles and kick her way out of it.

Ada fell back down on top of Patience with nothing between them.

Patience could not focus her mind. All she could feel was skin everywhere and she had never realized how sensuous it could be. She wondered if this was how people usually felt on their wedding night. If so, she finally understood why one might want to get married.

She wanted to touch everywhere, all at once, and wished she had enough hands to do so. Her mouth returned to Ada's breast, and the other girl pressed against her, thrusting herself at Patience. At the same time she stoked down Patience's body with a single finger, leaving off at Patience's belly and cupping her breast in one small hand. Patience bucked as Ada found her nipple and rolled it between her thumb and finger. In response Patience sucked harder and

Ada moaned again, louder, and threw her head back. This took some of her weight off Patience, and gave her room for her hand to move further down.

Tonguing Ada's nipple, Patience reached between their bodies and touched Ada's sex lightly. The liquid warmth nearly undid Patience, and she could feel Ada's hips lift toward her hand.

Rolling onto her hip, Patience lay the girl down on her back and raised her head from Ada's breast to look at her fully. She was glorious. Pale and glowing and Patience had to kiss her again. At the same time her hand stroked upward from the girl's thigh, skimming between the slender legs and touching carefully. She didn't want to hurt Ada and she didn't know what she was doing, but the sounds the dark-haired girl made encouraged her to keep exploring. One finger crept into the wettest part of her and sank to the first knuckle and Ada's hips bucked. Patience pushed slightly further and felt a blockage. She didn't know what it was, but explored with her fingertip. Carefully she slid a second finger in and moved them together, but the barrier worried her so she pulled them back and resumed stroking between the folds.

Ada's breathing was heavy as Patience moved, and her hips began thrusting in time with Patience's strokes. Her hands were still fumbling around Patience's body but they became slower and lackadaisical. Patience used her other hand to knead Ada's breast, while she sped up her stroking. Ada moaned continuously, jerking her hips faster as Patience's touch became firmer and she grew more confident.

Ada cried out and Patience felt a new flush of wetness cover her hand, warmer and more fluid. She kept stroking but let her touch lighten until Ada stopped jerking against her and then kissed the girl firmly.

Ada pulled down on Patience's back until she was almost fully covered by the larger girl. There was no space between them as Ada kissed Patience harder, and this time her tongue was the one that entered Patience's mouth. It felt so right, so familiar and yet she'd done nothing before that felt similar. Patience's cheeks burned as she remembered the feel of her fingers reaching inside Ada, somewhere no one had ever been. Her breathing quickened and Ada resumed her investigation of Patience's body. Like the other girl, Ada seemed to want to touch everything. She tasted Patience's nipple and Patience understood where Ada's moans had grown from. Did anything ever before feel that astounding? Were bodies meant to feel like that?

Patience moaned and moaned again as Ada's hands touched her full expanse. Somehow Patience was on her back and she didn't remember turning over. Ada's legs straddled her hips and she could feel wetness from Ada's sex touching her stomach. She rolled her head back as Ada took as much of Patience's breast into her mouth as could fit and then returned to sucking on her nipple. Her other hand stroked Patience's hips and thighs and reached just between her legs to skim over something that made Patience nearly pass out. She realized that was what her touch must have felt like to Ada and her fingers dipped between Ada's legs, wanting to reach that spot again but Ada grabbed her hand and pulled it away.

She felt rebuffed and looked away from Ada but the smaller girl shifted her head until she caught Patience's eyes.

"Let me first. I need to think."

Ada smiled and kissed Patience until she forgot to feel ashamed. When Patience smiled into Ada's mouth, the girl rocked towards her and began to inch down Patience's body, kissing as she went. She momentarily paused at Patience's breasts, tasting each one in turn and then continued to kiss down to her stomach and further, past crinkly hair to the juncture of Patience's legs. She stopped and looked at where she was, using her hand to push Patience's legs apart so she could see better.

Patience's face burned, though only part of it was from embarrassment. A small portion of her mind was sure no one was supposed to be looking at her there, but the rest of her was anticipating what Ada would do next.

The girl's fingertips lightly stroked Patience, pushing the hair aside and peering closer. Ada bit her lip, apparently lost in thought. Involuntarily, Patience's body jerked when Ada stroked the right place and she let out her breath with a sigh. Then Ada bent down and kissed Patience in that same spot, then touched it with her tongue. Patience almost flew off the bed. Nothing had ever felt like that. She wasn't sure she could survive it.

Ada stroked again, more firmly now that she was sure of herself. Her tongue swirled around Patience's sex. The heat and wetness were everywhere. Patience felt the warm muscle inside her and then it withdrew, repeating a number of times until Patience's eyes were screwed tight and she didn't know which way was up. Then it returned to the first spot and ran in circles around her.

Patience couldn't catch her breath. She never wanted to breathe again if it would make this go away. Something built up in her and she lost control, straining to meet Ada's tongue time after time. A bright explosion caused Patience to see stars but she didn't care. All she wanted was for Ada to stay right where she was until finally something cascaded within her and she cried out louder than she had ever done before.

When her vision cleared, Ada was watching her, looking quite pleased with herself. Patience put her arms around Ada's shoulders and lifted her so she could reach her mouth. She could taste a salty flavor that she knew was her own essence and beyond that something that was quintessentially Ada.

She'd never felt so at home.

For the rest of the night the girls took turns exploring each other's bodies, and resting and giggling together in between. In the morning Patience couldn't remember what they had talked about, but she felt she knew Ada better than she knew herself. She certainly knew Ada's body better than she knew her own. She had a vague memory of Ada admitting to reading a book her father had hidden away, and that was where she got the idea to try her mouth on Patience, an idea for which she was thoroughly thanked several times.

She had no idea when they had finally fallen asleep, but when she woke up Ada was tangled around her, breathing deeply and smiling in her slumber. Patience could feel the corresponding smile on her own face and lay there watching the girl until her eyes opened and their gazes met.

Patience's breath was taken away as she saw the happiness, and perhaps a small measure of vulnerability in the brighter light of day. Patience tightened her arms around the smaller girl, who buried her face in Patience's shoulder and then gave it a kiss. She started to kiss Patience's mouth but just then Patience's stomach growled.

Ada giggled until her own gave a corresponding rumble. She sat up, the bedclothes falling from her unashamed form and Patience's breathing hitched in response. Ada poked at her and then stood up, stepping into her dress but ignoring her shift on the floor. She reached down and tossed Patience's dress at her.

"Get up. We're going to find breakfast." She saw the gleam in Patience's eye and added "the food kind. In the kitchen," before Patience could get any ideas.

Trying not to pout, Patience pulled her own dress on, though she did step into her drawers first. Even with just the two of them, and certainly no secrets between them after the night, it felt a little immoral to have no underclothes on at all.

CHAPTER THIRTEEN

ADA DUCKED outside to collect eggs from the hens while Patience set water to boil for tea and took out a bag of oats and a box of cinnamon for oatmeal. She had no idea how to make oatmeal, but the cook always added cinnamon and sugar. She looked for sugar but couldn't find any so she asked about it when Ada came back in.

"I am looking for sugar," she said. "I checked the pantry but did not see any."

Ada shrugged. "There's only a tiny bit left. Perhaps enough for a few cups of tea, but no more than that. I'll sweeten the oatmeal with raisins."

Patience thought about it. "I could go to the village and get some more," she offered. "No one there knows me."

Ada winced. "I don't think that's such a good idea. Mr. Welsh will bring some eventually. We can do without for now. Besides, I don't have a lot of money left," she admitted. "We'd better save it for something we really need."

Tactfully, Patience agreed. "How often does Mr. Welsh come to check on you?" she asked.

"It's sporadic. When he can get away without anyone noticing. And he can't bring too much at a time or it would be obvious he was making deliveries. He's as careful as I could wish."

Ada still seemed uncomfortable so Patience changed the subject.

"Could you show me how the things work, upstairs?" she asked. Curiosity thrummed through her when she thought about all the objects in the workroom. "I do not mean how to run them, I learned enough about that yesterday, but how were they made? I have yet to see the inside of a clock, even. Father has one and Mason took it apart once, but I did not get a good look. I was forbidden to touch it, even to wind it. It is the one task Father does for himself."

Ada brightened. "Of course. We can go as soon as we eat. Father's made so many wonderful things. And I know how he did most of them. Except there are a few that are a big mystery."

"Perhaps we could try to make something ourselves, I have never made anything before, if you do not count embroidered samplers." Patience made a face. "I so hate to embroider. Unendingly tedious and requires no thought. A clockwork trinket is ever so much more interesting."

Ada spooned oatmeal into two bowls, added a

sprinkle of cinnamon and a handful of raisins to each and set them on the table. Patience stirred her bowl as Ada put a few hard boiled eggs in a saucer between them and poured tea. She noticed that Ada didn't use any sugar from the nearly empty packet she brought out, so she didn't either. The tea was strong with no milk and no sugar, but she resolved to smile and say she liked it best that way, should Ada inquire, though she usually added enough sugar to make her mother frown.

At home it would never have occurred to her that they could run out of anything, there always seemed to be too much. Too much food, too many new dresses, definitely too many dull visitors. She had never understood scarcity until her adventure on the road and she hoped never to do so again. There must be a way to get more supplies from the village without worrying Ada. She'd have to think about it.

The first thing Ada did when they reached the workshop was to name the tools that lay around the room. Other than tweezers, Patience didn't recognize much, but she was amazed at the variety. They ranged from the tiniest screwdriver, no longer than her smallest finger, to great sets of spanners, with everything in between.

"I see how it makes sense," she said, when they'd gone through everything, "to have so many tools so you can make things in a range of sizes. But would it not be easier to use the same size of screws or cogs, even in bigger things? Will they not work the same way no matter the size?"

Ada smiled. "The difference is in the power. The

bigger the spring, and the tighter you can turn it, the more powerful the device will be. If I used the same size works in the beast as, say, in the cat, then his legs would only move as much as the cat's, and his roar would be as quiet as the cat's meow. It wouldn't be powerful enough to scare away a fly. And if I used a beast-sized work in the cat, it would stick out the back and leap instead of walking and burn out very quickly. My father always stressed using the correct tool for the correct job and that applies to every part."

Patience considered this. "What if we put an even bigger clock inside the beast? Could we make him do more things? Could he bite, like the dog statue, and leap on people?"

Ada bit her lip. "I don't understand how Father made the dog bite, I don't think I could do that. But yes, I think we could improve the beast. It might be more useful if it had fewer limitations. We could make it scarier. I wonder if adding a second clockwork to control big movements, while the current one could do the smaller actions and the sound..." She started pulling things out of drawers and laying them out on the counter where most of the tools were, forgetting about Patience entirely.

She looked up again when Patience laughed. "I did not mean for you to start right now. I just mean sometime. You were going to show me how things worked. Then maybe I could help you with the beast."

Ada blushed. "Sometimes I get carried away," she mumbled, looking away from Patience.

Patience went to her. "And it is very charming." She touched Ada under the chin and raised her head so she was looking at Patience. "We will work together," she stated, and leaned in to kiss Ada softly.

The girl's arms went around Patience and she hugged her, kissing her enthusiastically.

Patience's heart rate increased and she pulled slightly away. "Later," she promised the other girl. "Show me how the cat works."

Ada gave her a small smile and fetched the cat, turning it upside down to show where the fur pulled away to reveal a tiny door. Inside was a jumble of what Patience recognized as gears and cogs and wires. It looked like a mess to her, but Ada pointed to each part and explained its function. She used the smallest screwdriver to take it apart so Patience could see exactly what made the legs move and what parts were for the cat's voice and what made it vibrate slightly when petted. It was amazing that something so small should have so many different pieces and that all were necessary to the function. Patience revised her estimate of Ada's skill. This cat was no toy, it was a work of art and if Ada had made the beast similarly, she wasn't just a clever girl, she was some kind of mechanical genius.

"What if one part stops moving?" Patience asked.

"It would mostly depend on which part. If the mechanism that made the cat meow didn't work, it wouldn't affect the rest of it, but if the main spring stopped the cat would do nothing." Ada put all the pieces back without hesitation; dozens of pieces in only a few moments, and Patience was amazed all over again.

Ada started the cat moving and it meowed, walked across the table and then curled into a ball and purred when Patience stroked it. It was the same motions she'd seen the first time she was in the workroom, but now that she knew how complex it was, the work that went into each tiny movement, she was astounded. "I wonder if you could control the movement somehow," she mused. "Not just in a straight line, but if you could tell it to go left or right and when to stop and go."

Narrowing her eyes, Ada considered the cat. "It's possible. There isn't a lot of room in there for other functions. But if we made a bigger one. A dog perhaps, that would have more room inside."

"Or we could try on the beast. That is much bigger and must have lots of empty places," Patience suggested. "And then if we needed to scare anyone else off, we could make the beast go up and roar in his face. That would be terribly effective. Not that I think anyone else will ever come," she added hastily, not wishing to frighten Ada. "But just in case."

Instead of frightened, Ada looked excited. "I never thought of that. I'm just used to Father's creations running through their paces by themselves. But if we could make it move where we wanted, it would be so much better." She hugged Patience again. "You're a genius."

Patience blushed. She didn't feel like a genius, she had no idea what exactly was running through Ada's mind and she wouldn't be able to offer any real help tinkering with the invention, but just maybe her ideas would let her be Ada's assistant. She'd always been told to stop expressing her ideas, but that hadn't stopped her from having them.

Ada was the first person in years who wanted Patience to use her mind, and was actually excited by it. She felt warm and wanted, both feelings new to her. She resolved to try as hard as she could to understand the things in that room, so she would be useful to Ada and could stay with her indefinitely.

"What are you thinking about now?" Ada asked, noticing Patience's faraway look.

"I was daydreaming," Patience admitted. She wouldn't tell Ada about these particular desires. It was too soon.

Ada smiled. "Help me bring the beast upstairs so we can start redesigning it."

"You should give it a name. It is similar to a pet, is it not? And it would be easier to call it something other than 'the beast' or 'the creature.'"

"I never thought of that either," Ada responded. "I haven't talked to anyone about it, so there was no need to name it. But perhaps you're right. What should we call it?"

Patience giggled. "Call it something like Daisy. It could be a girl beast."

Ada wrinkled her nose. "I think it's a boy beast. I didn't give it teats."

Patience had never heard anatomical parts being referred to so frankly and she blushed again.

It took Ada a moment to notice Patience's shocked look and then she poked Patience in the side, in a place she had discovered was quite ticklish.

"You're such a city girl!" she exclaimed.

"Mother says if there is no euphemistic way to refer to something, then not to mention it at all. There are a great many things Mother never mentions," Patience explained.

"Father says to call things what they are. Otherwise people get confused," Ada countered.

"Your father sounds a lot more sensible than my parents," Patience decided. "I will try to be as clear. But it may take some time."

"Let's call it Frank. Maybe that'll remind you about clarity."

Patience grinned. "Let us retrieve Frank and begin the surgery."

Halfway up the stairs, Patience decided Frank was heavier than he looked. "You ought to give him the ability to walk up and down stairs. Then we shall not need to do this again."

Ada nodded. "That should be possible, if I can control the legs to follow a pattern. I did give him bendable joints. I want to design it so he goes in a direction until he's told to stop or change. Otherwise I would have to control each step separately, and it would be more trouble than it's worth."

Once Patience had helped get Frank into the workshop, and had a look inside, she decided she'd better leave Ada to work. "I'm not going to be much help here. I think I will go down to the garden and see if there is anything ready to pick." She didn't know much more about gardens than about creating monsters, but she figured it had to be easier to understand.

Without looking up, Ada answered, "Some of the squash should be ripe, but that's probably all. It's the end of the season and too cold for much to grow."

Patience went over the contents of the pantry in her mind. There didn't seem to be enough food there to last Ada nearly through the winter, much less both of them.

Ada glanced up and must have seen Patience's worried expression. "All the food is stored away for the winter. There's always far more food than I can eat. I can and pickle and make jams. That's why I'm out of sugar, most of it went into jam. It's all in a cellar under the kitchen. I can show you later."

Patience let out a sigh of relief. "I can find it. You just keep... tinkering. I will put lunch together and call you when it is ready."

"Thank you." Ada said, sticking her head back into the opening in the beast. Patience watched for a moment, smiling at Ada's enthusiasm and then removed herself downstairs to do as she'd said.

"Ada." Patience called up the stairs for the third time. As with the two previous, there was no answer. She knew she was loud enough to be heard, even from the landing on the ground floor but the lack of response encouraged her to pile the sandwiches and tea onto a tray and carry it up the two flights of stairs.

She worried a bit that Ada might not be feeling well, as she hadn't responded to her calls, but was amused instead at the sight of her friend sitting cross legged on the floor, her skirt spread around her quite covered by hundreds of metal pieces. There were piles of cogs in different sizes and dozens of springs and far more bits than Patience could name, despite her lesson that morning. Ada was bent over something, holding it in one hand, using the other to screw a tiny screw in place. Patience noticed a few more sticking out from between Ada's pursed lips, something she'd seen dozens of dressmakers do with pins, but this was far more entertaining.

"I know my cooking is not spectacular, but surely it will taste better than metal screws," she quipped.

Ada's head jerked up and the screws fell out of her mouth into her lap. "Damnation," she said.

"Ada!" Patience exclaimed.

Cursing was something only drunks and vagabonds and sailors did, or so her books said.

Ada laughed at her surprise. "Don't worry. It's just what my father used to say when something wasn't going where he wanted it. I guess I picked up the habit." She seemed to think it was funny and Patience smoothed out her features. "Why didn't you call?" she said, looking at the tray of food in Patience's hands.

"I did. Three times. You ignored me." She placed the tray on one of the only spots on the counter that wasn't hidden under tools and bits of metal.

"Oops," Ada shrugged, seeing the chaos she'd spread through the workroom. "I think I got carried away." She put the device in her hand down and carefully sorted the objects scattered over her dress into piles of like materials. Patience extended a hand and helped pull her up. "Why didn't you use the dumbwaiter for the tray?" she asked.

Patience blushed. "I never considered it. It would have been more sensible than the stairs. Though moving the shelves away seems troublesome. We should shift those if we plan to use the contraption again," she suggested, knowing there would be a next time. "Apparently you inherited more than cursing from your father. Such as a tendency to forget meals?"

Ada had the grace to look a little embarrassed. "Did I forget to mention that part?" she asked, innocently.

Patience bit her lip to keep from laughing at her. "I forgive you. I made sandwiches. I brought up a ham from the cellar."

"Oh good. I love ham sandwiches." Ada wiped her hands off on her skirt and Patience made a mental note to leave a basin and pitcher of water up there, if, as she suspected, there would be more meals in the workroom.

"There's a table and chairs in the next room if you'd like to sit while we eat." Ada suggested. "That's where I used to drag Father to get him away from here for ten minutes. Otherwise he'd eat with a screwdriver in one hand and continue working as he chewed."

Patience giggled at the image, as she could easily picture Ada in the same situation. She picked up the tray again and followed her friend to the promised table and chairs.

This began a pattern that formed the next several weeks. In the morning Ada would work in the workshop, trying and testing new ways to make the beast move. Most of them didn't work at all, but small successes were celebrated. Patience learned enough about meal preparation to manage lunch, though Ada prepared dinner, as real cooking was still beyond Patience's experience. She would do whatever she was assigned, chopping vegetables or stirring soup, happy to be of assistance. She also took over the garden, weeding it regularly, brought in the last of the season's produce, and then prepared it for winter following Ada's instructions. She even learned how to do some simple work on the devices, under Ada's direction, and she grew to comprehend how the simpler systems worked. Ada was still light years ahead in her understanding.

In the afternoons they tidied the house, which took a surprisingly short amount of time. They kept to a few rooms and Ada's father had invented all sorts of time-saving devices. The crank that produced hot water was just the beginning. There was a machine, the round one that Patience had seen her first time in the workshop, that went around and around a room sucking up dust and dirt on the floor. She set it going and then left it alone to complete the job. She went back in a while to find the room clean and simply moved it to the next room. It worked on rugs as well as bare floors and Patience guiltily remembered the hours the housemaids spent washing floors and banging dust out of rugs. It was the first time she had ever considered how hard the servants must work. If those women had access to Ada's father's inventions, they wouldn't need to waken so early or go to bed so late. She wished she could send one back for them.

She did mention to Ada how much it would help though.

Ada said, "Father already patented this one. He wants to produce more of them. Hundreds. It will require a factory and to do that he'll need investors. That's the part he isn't terribly good at," Ada admitted. "He needs a partner who arranges for that sort of thing."

Patience noticed that Ada always spoke of her father in the present tense. Ada still believed that he was going to come back some day, and although Patience was skeptical, she made sure never to express that where Ada might see.

There were other devices to wash clothes and dry them quickly, to suck dust from the air, leaving less to fall upon furniture and knick-knacks, so they didn't need to do much dusting. There was even something that would chop a bunch of vegetables with the turn of a crank, making meal preparation faster. He really was a brilliant man, whether he came back or not.

After the house was clean the girls would sit together and read or play cards and talk about anything that came into their minds. That was Patience's favorite time of day. It wasn't that the discussions were always riveting, sometimes they were almost silly. But having someone to listen to and connect with, someone who enjoyed when Patience had an idea or an opinion, even one that was contrary to her own, was so novel that Patience couldn't get enough of it.

Then there were the times when they tossed the books aside and went to bed before dinner, getting up later to snack only if they were hungry. The physical contact was so new to Patience that she found it overwhelming at times, but she always craved more of it.

There were no rules in Ada's house. They got up when they chose, took breaks when they felt like it. Ate meals of whatever they put together and never worried about using the correct forks or sitting properly at table. Eating standing up at the workshop counters could be fun too, as long as Patience could get Ada to put down the tools long enough to get the food into her. It was all so amazing that Patience treasured every day.

The only thing she worried about was the stock of food, which were getting noticeably lower, and Ada mentioned that she had run out of this gear or that spring and had to take some older devices apart to salvage its bits. Mr. Welsh hadn't come for several months, and Ada didn't know why. Usually he was more regular than that.

"But if he's having a particularly busy winter, or if Calvin, his son, is being especially nosy, then he might not be able to get away long enough to buy what we need. He can't do it in the village because people would notice. So he has to take a cart to the bigger market in Eastbourne, and that takes time. We'll be fine though, there's still dozens of jars of pickles and jams, flour and oil and dried fruit and a few hams. And I can kill a chicken or two if I have to.

Besides, it's almost time to start planting and then we'll have so much food we shall have a feast!"

She didn't seem to be putting on a brave face for Patience's comfort; she really did seem to think there was lots of food yet. Patience supposed Ada had a better idea of what was needed than she did so she put it out of her mind.

The weather did soon start to get warmer, and one day, right after lunch, Ada declared it time to start working on the garden.

"First we have to go clear away any weeds that have grown through the winter, and then turn the soil and plant seeds." She showed Patience how to use yet another invention to soften and stir the soil up, with an attachment to poke holes for dropping the seeds into. It certainly looked easier than crawling around on her knees the way her cook had at home. And there was another crank and hose by the well, so watering was a simple task. She was amazed at how fast the first seedlings poked their shoots out of the ground.

"Does it always go so quickly?" she asked, as she carefully weeded around the proto-vegetables.

"If the weather is good it only takes a few weeks for the first crops to be ready. Some of them will take a lot longer though, and some we won't plant until full summer. We'll have a variety."

Patience took a deep breath. "I have been thinking about something. You keep saying there is always extra food. Even with two of us eating, there will be extra." She paused and Ada waited for her to continue. "What if I took some of the extra to the market to sell? That way we could get a bit of money and I can shop for the things we require."

Sugar was long gone, and flour was becoming scarce. There was meat though; once the small animals had seen the shoots growing, they had come back to the garden and the snare traps. Patience had learned how to skin them and cook the meat, and had even learned to preserve the furs so they could be used to fill in bare places on Frank's body. It wasn't something she enjoyed though, not like working in the garden. She was surprised to realize that she actually enjoyed getting dirty. Maybe because she hadn't been allowed to for so long.

Ada shifted uncomfortably. "We do need a few things, but what if someone sees you and wants to know where you've come from?"

"If I go through the woods, and come out somewhere far from here no one will know. I promise not to talk to anyone about where I live; I can ignore them if they ask. I will not say anything about you or about ever having been here. I can find out where Mr. Welsh is too, why he has not come."

Ada nodded slowly. "If you're sure no one will know. We do need some things. Anyway, it'll be a little while before we have anything worth selling. There's a cart down in the cellar that you can use to carry the food, and to bring things back. But just the regular things, flour and sugar and such. There's nowhere to buy gears and springs in town. We'll have to wait for Mr. Welsh for all that."

They didn't have to wait long, two days after Patience made her proposal, Mr. Welsh came to the door with bags full of supplies. There were some of the pieces Ada wanted, though not enough of anything. "I'm sorry I couldn't come earlier," he explained. "I was ill, and then Calvin was. I couldn't leave him. I'm terribly sorry. I hope you were okay."

Ada smiled and hugged him. "We were just fine." She gestured for Patience to come forward. The man started, he hadn't noticed her hanging back in the kitchen doorway. "This is my friend Patience," she took Patience's hand and pulled so they were standing next to each other. "And this is my father's friend, Mr. Welsh. He's brought some gears for me, and some sugar and things." Patience smiled at the man, partially because she knew Ada liked him and partially because she knew which supplies Ada considered more important.

"I am so pleased to meet you," Patience said, inclining her head slightly.

Mr. Welsh's face still registered surprise, and a little worry. Clearly he hadn't expected anyone but Ada to be there.

"Patience has been staying here since before winter." Ada explained. "She helped me with a little problem." Ada related the story about the men and how they'd scared them off.

Mr. Welsh listened carefully and seemed displeased. "I do wish you'd come and stay with me, just until your father returns. I don't like the idea of you here alone."

"But I'm not alone, not anymore." Ada reminded him. "Patience is here, and she's helping with everything. She's even going to take some things to market so we can earn some money and I can pay you for all the things you've brought for me." She was so earnest that Patience smiled at her. Mr. Welsh didn't seem much comforted though.

"Well, you know the offer is open. I must be getting back. Calvin was asleep but he's if he wakes he'll wonder why I'm not there. Goodnight, girls." He hugged Ada and shook Patience's hand, quickly ducking through the front door into the moonless night, knowing the hour and the darkness would hide his presence at the beast's house.

Ada seemed happy as Patience helped her put things away. "I knew there was a reason he was away so long. I'm so glad he's alright."

"I am not sure he was very happy to find me here." Patience mentioned.

Ada hugged her. "Don't worry, he just doesn't adapt to change very easily. And he doesn't know anything about you. Give him a few more visits and he'll love you too."

Patience's eyes opened wide and she stared at Ada. "You love me?" she whispered, wanting it to be true. She knew how she felt about Ada, but she hadn't considered that her friend might love her back.

"Of course I do, silly." Ada seemed to think that not loving her was a ridiculous idea, but as far as Patience knew, no one except her brother had ever loved her. She guessed her parents and sisters might, but that was from family obligation. And no one had ever said the words to her. Tears streamed silently down her face until Ada turned back from the sack she had been laying on a shelf and gasped.

"What's wrong?" Ada demanded, looking close to tears herself. "What happened?"

Patience tried to swallow her tears but she couldn't stop them.

Ada took a step back. "I shouldn't have said that. I'm sorry. I didn't know it would make you sad," she wailed.

Patience shook her head and grabbed onto Ada's arms, pulling her close and kissing her. She tasted her own tears and Ada's as well as she tried to show Ada how much it meant to her. It was a few minutes before she broke away. "I love you," she choked out. "I love you so much that I have no words for it. But I did not know that you felt the same. I was so scared to say anything."

"Silly." Ada whispered again, but this time the word sounded like an endearment. "Of course I love you. You're so beautiful and you aren't scared of anything, like I am, and you are so happy to talk to me about anything. Why wouldn't I love you?"

Patience gave up trying to explain and took Ada's hand. Ignoring the rest of the supplies lying on the floor of the pantry, she led the girl to the room they now shared and lay her down on the bed. She kissed every inch of skin she could reach and memorized the little sounds and gasps of breath each touch elicited. She never wanted to go anywhere else; she felt sure she would stay in this house with Ada forever.

CHAPTER FOURTEEN

THE VILLAGE market occurred on the first Tuesday of each month. Once the garden had produced enough surplus to be worth selling, the girls got up before dawn to prepare. They chose the best-looking vegetables, washed them and tidied leaves and stems so they presented their best face. Patience wore a simple dyed wool dress and left her hair down, as Ada explained that unmarried girls usually didn't put their hair up until they were officially classified as spinsters by the old biddies who controlled the spread of gossip in town.

Patience borrowed boots that were in better shape than her own, and finished the outfit off with a light wool cloak. Her goal was to seem like a simple farm girl, and Ada reminded her to speak in a more relaxed manner than she usually did, and to use contractions. It went against everything she had been taught by her mother and deportment tutor, and she relished practicing the transition.

"Good luck." Ada said, kissing her goodbye.

Patience paused with the front door just slightly open so she could make sure there was no one in sight. Quickly, she lifted the sacks containing her vegetables into the cart, which they'd hidden behind a hedge near the front door, and accepted a small bag of sandwiches for her lunch.

It was still chilly in the morning and she planned to take a very roundabout route and emerge from the woods on the far side of town where no one would trace her back to Ada's home. The sun was just peeking over the horizon and she clutched the cloak closed as best she could while needing both hands to push the cart. She entered the woods and traveled deep enough inside that no one would be able to see her from the town or the road that ran near it.

She ought to have practiced pushing the cart in the forest before, as it was a much bumpier walk than she had expected. At times she had to go quite far out of her way to find a gap in the trees that she and the cart could fit between, and roots and debris tripped her up a number of times. She hoped the produce wasn't getting too bruised and decided to pad the cart better the following month.

Emerging from the woods right where Ada had suggested, Patience easily found the market square and pulled out a large cloth, which she lay down on the ground before starting to unpack her vegetables. There were a number of other women and girls doing the same, most of them dressed similarly to her. They came from the surrounding countryside, their farms could be as much as five or ten miles away, and some of the girls already looked exhausted as their day had begun many hours before Patience's.

"Hello," a few people greeted her, noticing a newcomer in their midst.

"Good morning," she answered. She had a story all planned, about where her farm was and why she hadn't been to town before, but no one asked.

A harried-looking man planted himself in front of Patience's kneeling form, where she was straightening bunches of herbs. "You 'aven't been before, d'you 'ave your market fee?"

Patience's eyes widened. Ada hadn't told her anything about a fee to sell her products. "Could you explain please, sir?" she knew she sounded too formal and tried to smile lessen the effect.

"Fee of thruppence for a place in the square, sixpence for a table," he explained.

She shifted uncomfortably. "I haven't the money yet. May I pay you at the end of the day? Or even a little later?" She hoped the man was willing to bargain.

He scrutinized her, and her wares, and nodded. "I'll allow fer it just this once. Next time bring the fee up front. I'm 'ebbet and I'll be back for it la'er."

Patience nodded, making a note to save the coins out for the next time. "Thank you," she told the man as he moved on to the next woman. She listened and heard a few others making a bargain like hers and felt better not to be singled out. Patience carried a shopping list in her cloak's inner pocket. Her plan was to sell as much as she could in the morning, and then ask someone to watch her stall while she bought what she could with the proceeds. Since she had arrived early she had a good place near the crossroads. People would see her offerings before they would see many others and she hoped they'd buy quickly and not spend all day browsing.

She would like to get home as soon as possible, knowing that Ada was worried.

A few townsfolk started arriving and then there was a small flood. Patience sold her greens and broad beans quickly, but the herbs were not selling as well. Ada had warned her that most housewives kept an herb garden, but that bachelors would come later in the day and they would be her best customers for those items.

She was friendly with the townsfolk, but didn't offer too much information about herself and most of them seemed too polite or otherwise disinclined to ask. Her prices were in line with the other sellers, and a new face was always welcome in a small town, so much of her groundcloth was bare by midday. She sat on one corner to eat her lunch, making sure her skirts were laid properly and ready to jump up if any customers came. A few times she had been asked to keep an eye on neighboring stalls, so she felt safe approaching the woman next to her once she'd finished eating.

"Could you look after my things while I do a bit of my own marketing?" she asked, working to keep her accent softer.

The woman nodded, and Patience begun by

buying a sack of flour from her stall, without pricing it out. She'd already paid her market fee, and had held back three pence for the next month, but she still needed to be frugal in a way that she never had when shopping in her old life. Of course, she'd never bought flour and sugar before either, the cook took care of that, but she found she enjoyed a bit of bargaining, after listening to other people haggle to see how it was done, and she managed to find most of the things on her list without too much trouble. She even bought a light blue ribbon that she thought would match Ada's eyes perfectly.

By the time Patience was down to a few bunches of parsley and rosemary, she was exhausted and ready to head home. Her cart was heavier that trip, her purchases being of greater weight than the things she'd sold, and she wished she'd left earlier than she had. She entered the woods in the same place she'd emerged and, despite her exhaustion, took a route through the deeper woods, pausing every so often to make sure she couldn't hear anyone following her. She didn't know why they would bother, but she'd promised Ada that she would be extremely careful and so she was.

The sun was just setting by the time she saw the house through a gap in the trees, and her arms felt ready to fall off. Still, she looked around her, making sure no one was near before pushing the cart right to the front door, unlocking and starting to toss things inside. Ada joined her immediately, she must have been peeking out a window to see Patience arrive, and together everything was transferred into the house and the cart stored away in only a few minutes.

Only once the door was closed behind Patience did she greet Ada with a kiss. "That was rather more exhausting than I had expected," she said.

Ada grinned. "I have supper ready, and then we can move everything to the pantry. You look like you did well."

"Nearly sold out. You were right though, the herbs probably weren't worth the bother. I will take fewer next time. No one wanted them until the end of the day." She followed Ada into the kitchen where a pot of stew was bubbling away on the stove and bowls were already waiting to be filled. She had snagged the sack of sugar, and they enjoyed sweetened tea with their dinner, a treat they hadn't had for a while.

One month later, Patience retraced her route to the market and set up her stall in the same place as before. This time she had the money ready when Hebbet came to collect. She didn't know if Hebbet was the man's Christian or surname, but she supposed it didn't matter. She had more vegetables this trip. Everything in the garden seemed to be ripe at once.

As she ate her lunch, a shadow fell over her, blocking the sun from her face. Prepared for customers she lay her apple down on her napkin and quickly rose to her feet. "Can I help you, sir?" she asked the young man who towered over her.

The boy smiled at her.

"My father sent me over to buy some things. He

specifically told me to look for a pretty blonde girl about my age, so that's what I did. Here's my list." He showed it to her and she put together the requirements, placing them in a small sack she'd brought for that purpose, since he didn't seem to have brought a basket like most of the shoppers. "I'm Calvin Welsh. My father is the blacksmith here, but he's a clock maker too."

He sounded proud of that, and Patience schooled herself not to react to the familiar name. Ada didn't like him, she'd made a point of saying a number of times, and her instincts said Ada would know best, but Calvin hadn't done anything to her so she'd give him the benefit of the doubt. It was certain his father had given Ada a great deal of assistance and Patience liked him enough for that alone.

"I'm Pate," she replied, handing the bag over. The girls had decided it wouldn't do any harm to use her own first name, but Patience sounded too formal for most farm girls. When she was born her sisters were too small to say "Patience" so they called her Pate, and the name had lasted through their childhood, before they decided it was too undignified to use a nickname. She was used to answering to it, so it was easier than trying to remember something totally new.

Calvin switched the bag to his left hand and held his right out toward her. She hesitated, but then rested her hand in his own, not sure if he would shake it or kiss it. She rather hoped for the former, but didn't react when he chose the latter. He clearly had ideas that were grander than usual in such a small town, perhaps he planned to move to the city and was practicing.

She retrieved her hand. "A pleasure to meet you." She had returned to the more formal manner of speech that she'd been trying not to use in town, but she wasn't completely comfortable with the way Calvin was staring at her and she preferred he think her chilly than interested.

Calvin nodded and paid what she requested without trying to bargain. "I have to get back to help my father. But I'm sure I'll see you again soon."

He walked away before she needed to reply, though he did look over her shoulder at her several times. She returned to her lunch but he kept intruding on her thoughts for the rest of the afternoon. There was something about him.

Patience didn't mention Calvin when she returned home that evening, having sold everything and even earned enough extra to pay Mr. Welsh for some of the supplies he brought the next evening. Without the need for him to carry more than the metal bits and bobs, he could secrete them in his pockets and say he was going out for a walk, so he was visiting more frequently, though always after dark. Ada was pleased she didn't have to rely upon him for everything, anymore, but she still expressed worry to Patience before each trip.

"Remember, don't come out in the town too close to here, and be more careful coming back. Someone is far more likely to see you then, when you're tired and want to get home." The habit of reclusiveness was so ingrained in her that this aberration made her fret about the same things every month.

Patience laughed and tugged at Ada's plait. "I'm always careful, you worry too much."

She knew Ada would spend most of the day staring out the window, waiting for her return rather than tinkering in the workshop like she did most non-market days. "Why don't you work on Frank today?" she suggested. Ada still hadn't worked out the control system to her satisfaction and kept putting it aside to think about it more while she tried other projects.

Patience was far out of her depth and her suggestions were generally met with "I tried that already."

By the fourth market day, Patience had established a routine and had begun to enjoy the trips. She loved Ada, but she wasn't used to only talking to one or two people and was surprised to find herself missing some of the more social aspects of her old life. The market allowed her to interact with lots of different people, without any of the behavioral rules that she'd hated.

Farm girls were not expected to 'be seen and not heard' and she was somewhat envious when she'd see a family marketing together, the parents teasing the children or vice-versa. She liked the children and took to keeping a small bag of sweets on her to hand out while their parents made a purchase, or just because they looked like they wanted one. She came to know most of the children, and some of their parents, by name and would call out greetings as they passed by.

It didn't hurt her business to be friendly either, she noted people specifically aiming for her stall. She was glad that she didn't have enough to sell to really impact the farm families' incomes. She was sure they needed the money from market day to get through the month, and although she and Ada weren't exactly well off, she still didn't want to hurt anyone by taking away from them.

The only thing that marred these expeditions was Calvin's presence. He stopped by every single market day, usually bought a few things and then stood around talking as long as he could get away with it. Although Patience greeted him cordially, she didn't linger to chat and was often grateful to whoever interrupted him.

"My father wishes to send me to university," he mentioned one day. "What do you think of that?"

Patience replied, "If you ask what is the good of education in general, the answer is easy; that education makes good men, and that good men act nobly."

He gaped at her, not recognizing the quote, and she turned away smiling. She wouldn't say what was truly on her mind, which was that Calvin was about the least-suited student she could imagine. He was vain and pretentious, but didn't seem to have much interest in thinking about anything but himself. And he certainly wasn't well read, or he would have recognized Plato.

The one time she had asked him what he liked to

read he scrunched up his nose. "I'm too busy to waste time on novels. I have important work to do in my father's forge."

As far as she could see, from his spotless clothes and thin torso, he wasn't doing much blacksmithing. Perhaps he was helping with the clocks. But when she mentioned to Mr. Welsh that she had met his son and that he spoke of helping his father, the man shook his head sadly.

"I wish he would. I have orders piling up and barely enough time to see to the clocks in the village as it is, much less to design anything new. My boy likes to talk big, but I'd be careful what you believe, if I were you."

Patience had figured that out already but Ada frowned and asked her about it later. "Is Calvin bothering you?"

"A little," Patience admitted. "I think he's mostly just talk, but he's spending more time at my stall than I like. I keep trying to gently suggest that he get on with his day, but he doesn't seem to realize that I wish him to leave."

Ada snorted. "Calvin wouldn't take a hint if you wrapped it around a rock and hit him between the eyes. Just tell him to leave you alone." She regarded Patience's figure languidly. "Though even that might not help. At least the brat has taste."

Patience blushed, but was pleased nevertheless and let Ada steer her to more interesting conversation.

She tried the suggestion at the next market day. When Calvin had purchased his vegetables, and brought her a posy of flowers from a different stall, she tried to send him away a little less obliquely. "I am sorry, Calvin, but I need to rearrange my stall. The carrots aren't selling as well as I'd like."

She figured he'd either leave or offer to help, but he just stood there while she bent down and sorted out the produce so the carrots were better displayed. As she started to rise he put his hand under her elbow and lifted her up. She did not like the smirk on his face so she stepped away from him and was pleased to see the nice couple who ran the town's only public house stepping up to her stall. She turned to greet them and pointedly ignored Calvin until he gave up waiting and left.

As she gathered her purchases together to place them in her handcart, Patience looked around carefully to see if anyone was watching as she entered the woods in her usual place. She thought she saw a flash of movement in the woods but waited and she didn't see it again so she went along as usual, keeping an eye and an ear out for anything out of place. She took a longer way through the woods than usual, too, just to be sure. It was dusk before she left the woods and headed quickly to the front door.

"I knew there was something funny," a low male voice sounded from behind her.

She whirled around and came face to face with Calvin, who was wearing a very satisfied expression. "What are you talking about?" she asked, her heart speeding up. She debated continuing to push the cart past the house and keep going until he lost her in the darkness but she realized that wasn't going to help.

"You live here. Don't you? You live with that... creature." His face bunched up unattractively as he regarded the curtained-off windows. "What are you? Its keeper or its mistress?" he asked.

Patience stared him down. "You know nothing about him," she stated, keeping her voice as calm as possible under the circumstances.

He shuddered. "I know that it's a filthy, evil thing and that anyone human who let it touch her would be sick. But..." he paused for effect, "I'm willing to look past that. I think it's time I was married, and I think you'd make the perfect wife. Once you're away from here."

Patience looked at him in shock. "I'm not going to wed you. I'm...not even old enough," she lied, trailing off uncertainly.

He leered at her, in the fading sunlight. His eyes lingered on her breasts and she hunched her shoulders forward, wishing it was still cool enough to be wearing a cloak.

"You certainly look old enough, and ripe enough, to me," he responded, not even bothering to raise his eyes to her face.

She could feel her face flush. "I do not wish to marry at this time."

This time he looked at her more speculatively. "Your wishes aside, I suggest that you consider my offer. If you should not, it may become known about your 'living arrangements.' I know you've made friends in town, imagine what they would think if they knew you were nothing but a doxy to a soulless creature?"

Patience's mouth dropped open in horror. "You actually think that I..."

Just then, an upstairs window opened and Patience could see the form of the beast neatly outlined. A ferocious roar wiped the leer off Calvin's face and he backed away. "I'll give you a month to make your choice. By the next market day you will agree to my proposal or you lose all your friends. And I wonder what the townsmen would think of a human woman living like that. They might even do something ... drastic. One month," he repeated, and then turned and quickly walked back towards the town, following the road.

Patience sagged against her cart as he walked away, and a moment later the front door jerked open. "What happened?" Ada exclaimed. "I couldn't hear, but he looked like he was threatening you."

Patience reached for her hand and squeezed it. "Let's go inside and I'll tell you everything."

CHAPTER FIFTEEN

ADA TURNED white and trembled as Patience told her about the visits Calvin had been paying to her stall, and his attempt to blackmail her into marrying him. She assumed it was fear that made the girl quiver. "Don't worry," she attempted to soothe Ada, "I'll think of something. I won't let him start spreading filthy rumors and no one will come." She put her hand on her friend's arm.

Ada blinked at her. "Of course we'll think of something. But he threatened…" she seemed to lose her voice as her mouth worked, attempting to produce words. "How dare he!" she finally cried, at a decibel Patience had never heard from her before.

Patience stared at Ada speculatively. "He thinks I'll marry him out of desperation," she said. "But he doesn't know that I'm not desperate, nor am I at all unhappy with my situation. Let's put everything away and we can make a plan over supper." She realized that Ada was furious with Calvin because he wanted to hurt her, and, despite the reason for it, it made her feel special, loved. Ada didn't seem to be worried about Calvin; she was offended on Patience's behalf.

"We could blow him up." Patience suggested, a forkful of boiled potato halfway to her mouth. They had been debating options for a while now, and they were starting to get a bit silly about it.

Ada took the suggestion literally. "We'd have to do it outside. I don't want Mr. Welsh's home damaged because his son is a cretin."

Patience nodded. "Whatever we do has to be something that won't hurt his father. It wouldn't be kind to repay him for his help by destroying his property."

"His son isn't property, and I wouldn't mind destroying him," Ada growled.

"Possibly something less drastic?" Patience thought about the intruders. "Can we scare him into leaving me alone?"

Ada sobered. "If we could get into his house to lay traps, but I don't know how we would do that without being seen by someone else in town. Their house is nearly in the middle of it."

"What if we waited until very late at night?" Patience suggested.

"That would help us remain unseen, but we would still need to get everything inside. And how can we convince Calvin that his house is haunted, or that there's a lion there that he never noticed before?"

"Frank. We'll only have to take Frank. If we use him to scare Calvin out of his mind, he won't be a threat to us. Especially if we make him think that the beast will tear him limb from limb if he so much as mentions it in town."

Ada frowned. "I still haven't worked out a control system yet. Not one sophisticated enough to take him on a long walk, nor to speak beyond roaring. I'd need to refine everything and I don't know if I can do it."

Patience smiled at her. "I have faith in you. And I'll help. Between us we should be able to come up with something. And Mr. Welsh told me today that he would be leaving for London two weeks from tomorrow. I know that doesn't give us much time, but it will keep him well out of it and in no danger of being hurt."

The girls neglected every other chore to spend the next two weeks trying out different ideas to improve Frank's mobility and refine small motor functions. After all these months, Patience had a much better idea of what was required to improve the devices upstairs, and it was she, playing with the lion's roar recording, who figured out a way to combine a speaking voice with the roaring, so it sounded like the lion was talking. She added a cone-shaped tube that one could speak into so a listener would think that Frank was speaking in response to something that was said.

"One of us will have to be there, maybe hiding a few feet back, but we'd have to be close enough to hear anything Calvin said," she explained, showing Ada what she'd created with a small version of a gramophone's cone from which the sound played. "You can whisper into it and the sound comes out much louder." She demonstrated. It was the first thing she had made that Ada hadn't helped with.

Ada hugged her. "That's perfect. I've got Frank moving around in small areas, but I'm still not sure how to power him to move as far as the town. Even if we wound him up numerous times, he would still be in danger of running down once we're in the house."

Patience examined him. "What if we didn't make him walk the whole way? What if we pushed him in the cart through the woods until we were almost there? Then we could wind him once to get into the house, and up the stairs, and a second time when we need him to perform."

Ada did some calculations on a sheet of paper where she'd been recording Frank's action times. "I'll have to see if he can do the stairs here first. If he can do that on one wind, it should be fine."

She wound the crank as far as it would go, and used her control box to steer the beast out the door, to the landing and down the stairs. On the way back up he wound down, but when she started at the bottom of the stairs with a fresh charge he made it all the way up and back to the workshop before stopping. "That's enough. We will have to pray that no one else sees us, and Calvin will need to be asleep or else we won't have time to wind him before the brat investigates the sound of him coming upstairs."

The footsteps did sound rather loud on the

wooden stairs.

"We could make him little furry booties so he's quieter," Patience suggested. "Some of the rabbit skins glued to the bottom of his feet to muffle the sounds."

"That might work, at least it will help. I hope Calvin is not a light sleeper."

Patience had other questions. "How are we going to get into the house? Won't the door be locked for the night? And what if the servants awaken?"

Ada shook her head. "Their housekeeper goes home at night, once Mr. Welsh and Calvin have finished dinner. They have a maid who comes in the morning, but they don't have any live-in servants. I had forgotten about the lock though. A clock maker's lock will be a good one. Clocks are valuable. I don't suppose you know how to pick locks?"

"Of course, it was one of the first things my deportment tutor taught me," Patience grinned. "Too bad neither of us ever considered a life of crime."

Ada smiled, but sobered quickly. "Mr. Welsh leaves tomorrow. We only have two nights, three at most to make this work. We have to think of something!"

But by the next night, neither had thought of a solution. As they lay in bed, feeling the time tick away, Patience rolled over and tilted her head. "Does the house have a back door?" she asked.

"It has a door into the kitchen, the same as here," Ada replied. "But the housekeeper will lock that door when she goes home."

"What if someone were already inside before she

went home? Hiding somewhere in the house? If I waited around back until she serves dinner, I could sneak into the kitchen and hide in the pantry until she leaves, then I could unlock the door for you."

Ada's expression exhibited doubt. "What if they catch you? What if Calvin catches you? It certainly wouldn't help the situation."

Patience bit her lip. "It's not like I want to do it, but I'm out of ideas and we are running out of time. It has to be tomorrow. And you're the one who has to control Frank, so I had better be the one in the house."

Both girls had tried the control on the beast, but Patience had trouble getting it going the right direction. Ada found it much easier.

Ada seemed ready to refuse but Patience broke in. "Besides, if I do get caught, I'll get caught, but if you get caught, they'll know you're here alone and everything will be ruined. Let me do this." She grabbed Ada's hands between her own. "I have to make it right again. Calvin is blackmailing me and I have to be part of the solution. It's important to me."

Ada slowly nodded. She didn't look happy.

Patience kissed her. "It'll be all right," she whispered, wishing she felt as certain as she sounded.

The next afternoon, Patience dressed in boy's clothes that Ada had found in one of the disused rooms and put her hair up under a cap. She wasn't a terribly convincing boy, but at a glance she might pass. She hugged Ada goodbye and darted into the woods. Her intention was to wait there until she was sure no one was on the streets, and then to sneak around Mr. Welsh's house to the yard in back. Ada had told her there was a window in the kitchen that she could peep through to see when the housekeeper, Mrs. Humphries, was out of the room. Then she'd let herself in, hide in the furthest corner of the pantry and hope no one locked that at night. She didn't think it was likely anyone bothered, but it was one factor she couldn't control. She'd wait there until Mrs. Humphries left, stay in the kitchen until she heard Ada knock three times on the back door and then let her in.

Ada would have to push the cart with Frank through the woods on her own, but she was strong and Patience had managed it loaded with produce and purchases, so they didn't think the beast's weight would be much of an issue.

The worst part of everything was waiting.

Patience made it to the garden without incident, though her stomach was trying to turn somersaults. She could see a pleasant-faced middle-aged woman working inside. Patience ducked down below the window and only looked up for a brief moment every so often to check if the woman was still there. Because it was summer, dinner would likely be served well before dusk, and she couldn't rely on darkness to hide her, she would have to be quick and silent. Finally she peered over the sill and saw an empty kitchen. Standing properly she took a second look to confirm that Mrs. Humphries wasn't just in a corner, but she was nowhere in sight. Taking a deep breath, Patience eased open the back door, praying it didn't creak. When she heard no reaction from the rest of the house she darted inside, closed the door gingerly, and crossed the kitchen to the pantry. There was no key in the lock and her heart beat fast as she tested the door to make sure it was open. A sound from the hallway startled her and she quickly threw the door open and ran inside, closing it behind her.

Then she waited.

There was no immediate response, so she felt sure that neither Mrs. Humphries nor Calvin had heard her entrance. She moved a few large sacks away from one of the corners and sat on the floor behind them, glad she'd left her skirts at home; it was much easier to secrete oneself in trousers. Rustling sounds in the kitchen let her know it wasn't yet time to emerge, though it felt like she'd been there for hours. At one point her heart almost exploded from her chest when the pantry door opened, and she held her breath as the older woman placed something on a shelf inside and closed the door without looking around. Patience waited for her heart rate to return to normal and forced herself to take calming measured breaths until she didn't feel like running for the woods.

Shortly after that there was the sound of a door closing heavily, and she could just hear a lock being turned. Finally. Patience counted in her head to five hundred and, when no other sound came she propped the pantry door open a crack so she would hear Ada's knock when it came. She wished she had something to do to occupy herself. The sun still shone through the kitchen window and she knew it would be a long time before Calvin would be asleep and Ada would come.

She conjugated Latin verbs in her head for a while, dismayed at how much she had forgotten. Then she started thinking about home, and what her parents would be doing. She wondered if they missed her, or were only embarrassed that she had disappeared after the announcement of her engagement. She suspected the latter. Maybe someday she would write to them to let them know she was safe. If she was. If their plan didn't work she would either have to marry Calvin or go home to marry Gabriel, if he would still have her. But that would leave Ada alone and at risk of Calvin's retribution. No, there was no choice. She couldn't leave Ada. It would simply have to work.

To distract her from that train of thought, she focused on Ada herself, her smile and her hair and her mannerisms. This was a much more pleasurable way to pass time, and she almost didn't hear when three knocks came softly on the back door. She peeked outside and was surprised to realize that it was fully dark.

Treading quietly to the door, she unlocked it and let Ada inside. She was preceded by Frank, in his booties. Ada handed her the voice box, which she would use while Ada controlled the direction of their beast. Ada threw her arms around Patience's waist, as it if had been more than a few hours since they'd last seen each other. Patience returned the hug and rubbed her back with the hand that wasn't holding the voice box.

"I left the cart in the back, under a tree. I hope no one notices it there," Ada whispered, barely audible even from inches away.

"I don't think Calvin has gone upstairs yet. At least, I haven't heard anything on the stairs," Patience responded. "How long do you think we'll have to wait?"

Ada shrugged. Patience could barely see her in the moonlight that came through the window. She hoped there would be more light when they tried to climb the stairs. "Do you have a candle or a lamp?" she voiced her worry. "How are we going to get Frank up the stairs in the dark?"

Ada produced a candle stub and matches from the pocket of her trousers. They were rolled several times at the cuffs and clearly miles too big for her, though Patience's fit relatively well. She thought Ada looked adorable, like she was dressed in her big brother's clothing for a fancy dress party.

She forced her mind back to their problem.

"We can light this to find the stairs, but I think we'd better blow it out before we ascend. I remember where Calvin's room is, and you can hold onto me and follow. Stay to the edge of the stairs, so they won't creak," Ada said.

They resumed waiting quietly until they heard Calvin's heavy steps on the stairs. "How long until he falls asleep?" Patience wondered.

"We had better give him an hour at least. He might be reading, though I don't remember him enjoying that as a boy." She consulted a pocket watch in the faint moonlight. "I'll sneak up quickly first to make sure there's no light under his door. Then I'll come down for Frank and you."

The girls watched the clock hands, which moved inexorably slowly. After a little more than an hour Ada stood and reached down for Patience, helping her to rise. She lit the candle and handed it to Patience, who led the way to the stairs. When they were standing by the first step, Ada lightly ran up and came down again a moment later. "No light," she whispered.

Patience blew the candle stub out and placed it out of the way at the very edge of the first step. Ada tightened Frank's clockwork, and he started walking up, slowly, with Ada guiding him from behind. Patience put her hand on Ada's back and followed her up the pitch black stairs. They paused at the landing as Ada made sure Frank was wound. Both took a deep breath and let it out in unison. Patience's stomach was tumbling and she sent a quick prayer to whomever was listening that this would work.

Then Ada reached for the second door on the left and threw it open, stepping behind Frank and directing him into the room.

When the door hit the wall behind it there was a reactionary gasp, and then the sound of fumbling, which turned out to be Calvin lighting the lamp beside his bed. He threw back the sheets and backed away as he laid eyes on Frank standing in the doorway. "What? Why?" he gibbered, sounding high-pitched and terrified. His back hit the wall and he pressed back against it. "Who are you?" Calvin managed.

Patience raised the soundbox to her mouth as Ada dropped the beast's mouth open. "You know who I am," she roared. She and Ada had practiced likely responses at home, so she would know what to say.

Calvin did not respond. He just looked more terrified. Patience peeked around the door and then drew back, continuing to talk into the box. Ada was on the other side of the doorway, and only the thin cord of the control unit connected her to Frank's body. It was completely hidden by his bulk from the front.

The beast roared and then Patience continued. "Do you think you can get away with blackmailing the girl? She is under my protection. You will not harm her. You will not speak to her. You will not enter her presence at any point. Do you understand?" As she listed off the rules, Ada made the beast raise his right paw to tell off each item on his claws.

Calvin squeaked as he saw the claws, which had been lengthened and filed until they were sharp and buffed, and gleamed in the lamplight.

"DO YOU UNDERSTAND?" Patience as Frank roared again.

A sharp ammonic scent came to Patience where she waited in the hallway. She heard Calvin stammer, "Yes." It was so quiet she could barely make it out.

"If you do not stay away from her, if you ever speak to her again, I will return. I will rend every limb from your body, and then I will use these claws," the claws wiggled to catch the light, "To tear the beating heart from your chest while you still breathe."

Ada made the beast take a few steps toward Calvin, who was now sobbing. Suddenly, Ada dropped the control and threw herself at Patience, pushing her a few steps into the dark hallway as Calvin came running out of the room. He half tumbled down the stairs, fiddled with the lock, threw open the front door, and fled into the night. He did not see either girl, or the cord that trailed behind the now-still creature. He must have thought the beast was chasing him, because as they hurriedly descended the stairs to see where he went, they could only make out a dark form running as fast as possible away from the town.

"Do you think he'll tell the police?" Patience asked. She was worried he'd find the local officers and bring them to the house.

"Police?" Ada asked, "In this town? We haven't any police force, this isn't London, or even Canterbury. There's only the Parish Constable here, and he'd be more afraid of Frank than Calvin was." She laughed. "Did you see the look on his face?"

Patience swallowed the fear that still rumbled through her and smiled. "He did look quite amusing. Did you notice that he wet his breeches?" she said.

"He didn't!" Ada cried, tears running down her face from laughing so hard.

Patience closed and locked the front door before anyone could see or hear them and come to investigate. "We'd better go home," she said, reminding Ada that they weren't quite safe yet.

They retrieved Frank and got him back into the

cart and through the woods. Once home, Ada steered him back to his cupboard. "In case we need him again," she told Patience, reaching up to pat the creature on the head.

They got ready for bed quietly, though Ada kept giggling every so often.

"Will we be safe?" Patience asked once they were in bed and the lamp blown out.

"Only time will tell," Ada replied, snuggling close.

EPILOGUE

MR. WELSH dropped by to bring Ada some supplies from London. "You know, the strangest thing happened while I was away," he remarked, over a cup of tea, holding a biscuit in his left hand. "When I got back from London, Mrs. Humphries told me that when she came to the house on Wednesday morning, the back door was unlocked and Calvin was nowhere to be found. She couldn't find anything missing, nor could I when I searched. And just this morning I got a letter from Calvin, from London, saying he had decided to enter the university there and would I please send the tuition money."

The girls looked at each other and then back to Mr. Welsh.

"The strange thing is, just last week he was telling me that he thought he'd stay here and get married.

He hasn't mentioned anything about university before, though I've offered to send him numerous times."

Patience couldn't resist. She cleared her throat and quoted, "But if you ask what is the good of education in general, the answer is easy; that education makes good men, and that good men act nobly."

Mr. Welsh joined her on the last line. "Ah, Plato's philosophy on education. Very apt."

Ada nodded seriously. "Clearly he came to the conclusion that London was the safes... I mean, the best place for him. I hope he does well there."

Mr. Welsh nodded. "Yes, perhaps you're right. I'm sure he'll find London to his liking; he may do well with a larger and less provincial audience. London is full of new surprises around every corner, practically." He put down his cup and finished his biscuit, brushing the crumbs from his trousers with his hand and depositing them on the saucer. "Thank you, girls. Do let me know if there's anything else you need. I'm sure I'll be seeing you in town soon, Patience."

They rose and let him out, watching through the window as he looked around carefully before turning in the direction of his house.

"Well, London. Isn't that something?" Ada remarked.

"A much better place for Calvin, lots of new surprises." Patience added. "Perhaps he will decide to stay there, once his schooling is through." She hoped he would anyway.

Ada giggled and poked her in the side, gathering the tea things onto a tray. "Act nobly indeed." She snorted.

Patience shrugged her shoulders. "It could happen," she responded, following Ada from the room and feeling the last of her anxiety drift away. She didn't know what they would do next, but they had lots of time to think about it.

Want more steampunk? Check out:

In 1899, a secret society tried to use a young woman to bring an ancient evil into the world. Twenty years later they will return to finish the job.

After the Great War, London is settling once more into the gentle routine of peacetime. The airships that once protected England's coast now ferry people back and forth across the Thames, the magically-inclined are free to return to their normal work, and those who seek treasures left behind by ancient civilizations are again free to explore. Dorothy Boone shunned a life of luxury to follow in her grandmother's footsteps by uncovering the mysteries of "the worlds that came before ours."

When a package explodes upon delivery to Lady Boone's townhouse, she is drawn into an unlikely alliance with her nemesis, Trafalgar of Abyssinia, to find the culprit.

They soon find themselves unraveling a plot that has left many of their allies dead and the rest in fear for their lives. A group of treasure hunters with a fiendish plot to take over England has begun eliminating its competition in order to fund an expedition to retrieve the last item they need for a summoning that will bring an ancient evil into our world. With no one else to trust, Trafalgar and Boone must put aside their differences and forge a partnership to stop their mutual enemy. If they fail, a world that still bears the scars of the Great War will be once again thrown into turmoil.

Welcome to the world of Trafalgar and Boone, a world where airships battled in a Great War that was fought by soldiers who utilized magic and summoned monsters to do their bidding, a world that they must defend by working together to stop an evil far greater than either of them could ever have imagined.

Employed by the military as an airship captain, Dice knows exactly as much as she needs to get her cargo from one field to the next. Information is fiercely regulated, and sharing of knowledge is punishable by death. Dice has no interest in learning until she begins an illicit romance with the engineer assigned to her ship. The romance is short lived when the man she loves is captured and Dice's crime comes to light.